What the critics are saying about Lawrence Schimel

"I wish I knew Lawrence Schimel's secret of getting so much character into so few words."

—Marion Zimmer Bradley

"Schimel is a respected editor and a widely-published writer of short fiction."

—The Advocate

Praise for
TWO BOYS IN LOVE

"Ringing with emotional truth, *Two Boys in Love* is sweet, sexy, and very romantic. Whether writing about New York, Madrid, or the world of the fairy tale, Lawrence Schimel deftly brings his setting alive with perfectly-chosen details."

—M.J. Pearson, author of *The Price of Temptation*

THE DRAG QUEEN OF ELFLAND

"Lawrence Schimel's short stories ring contemporary changes into the romances and märchen that comprise the blueprints of our literary heritage. Schimel's stories are both spry and sly, and the best of them are grounded in humor or pathos. Some of them are over almost before they start; this is good, for in both magic and desire there should always be more than meets the eye."

—Gregory Maguire, author of *Wicked*

"Schimel displays the clean prose, fresh eye and ticklish imagination that have brightened his star as both a writer and anthologist."

—Publishers Weekly

"Schimel has a wonderful knack for creating resonant images and covering complex emotional territory in few words."

—Outrage, Australia

"This collection of short stories by the accomplished Schimel possesses equal amounts of charm and chills. These are fairy tales on two levels—magic infiltrates the mundane and, through the gay sensibility, the mundane becomes magical. The author subverts the traditions of story-telling with a peculiarly queer perspective— lesbian and gay vampire tales, ghostromances and a snappy little story of Jesus wearing Calvins. Having already proved himself to be an astute editor of anthologies, Schimel shows great flair for the short story. These fanatasies are thoroughly entertaining and should, like their archetypes, stay with the reader long after the book is finished."
—The Sydney Star Observer, Australia

HIS TONGUE
"His stories...stimulate the mind as well as the body and break the traditional stereotypes of pornography to create a new erotic literature, tender and at the same time sexy."
—Diario 16, Spain

"This book of stories is indispensable for the nightstand of every reader."
—Shangay Express, Spain

TWO BOYS IN LOVE
stories of romance and desire

TWO BOYS IN LOVE
stories of romance and desire
by Lawrence Schimel

Seventh Window
Publications

Two Boys in Love © 2006 Lawrence Schimel

All rights reserved. Except for brief passages quoted in a newspaper, magazine, radio, or television review, no part of this book may be reproduced in any form or by any means, electronic or mechanical, including photocopying and recording, or by any information retrieval system, without permission in writing from the publisher.

This book is entirely a work of fiction. Though it contains incidental references to actual people, products and places, these references are merely to lend the fiction a realistic setting. All other names, characters, places and incidents are the product of the author's imagination. Any resemblance to actual persons, living or dead, events or locals is entirely coincidental.

First Seventh Window Publications edition: May 2006

Cover illustration © 2006 Michael Lyons – all rights reserved

Published in the United States of America by:
Seventh Window Publications
P.O. BOX 603165
Providence, RI 02906-0165

Library of Congress Control Number: 2006921547

ISBN-13:   978-0-9717089-4-5
ISBN-10:   0-9717089-4-0

Contents

The Book of Love	9
The Road to Love	23
Märchen to a Different Beat	31
Fag Hag	45
Season's Greetings	53
The Story of Eau	67
Occasion a Need	77
Water Taxi	85
The River of Time	97
Two Boys In Love	127
Can't Buy me Love	129
A Movie Date	137
Passersby	147
The Night is Young	153
Independence	159

The Book of Love

The Ramblas were even more crowded than usual, but that was no surprise today. Booksellers had their stalls set up all along both sides of that famous pedestrian walkway that leads Barcelona down to the Mediterranean, and throngs of people were desperate to browse the latest titles and find something appropriate to bring home to their loved ones. The flower sellers were likewise happy as could be, selling roses hand over fist as the day progressed. On Sant Jordi, the Saint's Day celebrating the Patron Saint of Catalunya, you were supposed to give a book and a rose to your lover and friends—a tradition begun by the Catalan Publisher's Association in the 1960's when April 23rd was declared the Dia del Libro to commemorate the deaths of both Cervantes and Shakespeare—and people were afraid to come home empty handed, at least here in Barcelona, as well as in many other cities up and down Spain's eastern coast.

My boss had given me the afternoon off from work, but I almost wished she hadn't, since Sant Jordi always made me depressed. If I lived anywhere else in Spain, I wouldn't care, but I always felt so lonely and alone on Sant Jordi, watching the whole world go through this elaborate romantic ritual, while I had never once had a boyfriend when the day rolled around. Even if I happened to be dating a guy—which seemed a rare enough occurrence in my life although I had little trouble finding sex with other men, when I wanted it, either at the bars or the bathhouses or on the street—we always broke up before Sant Jordi, as if to spite me.

Still, I felt drawn to the Ramblas like everyone else, and since I had the afternoon off anyway I didn't resist; I probably would've taken a stroll down them, regardless, maybe stopping for a drink at the Cafe del Opera and watching who walked by. I was sure that various friends of mine were among the masses of people and that chance would let us run into one another. I was half afraid of running into my friends, too, since almost all of them were in relationships and I thought seeing them so contented together would only make me more depressed. But then, I wasn't sure if this feeling of intense loneliness, even while surrounded by so many people, was worse; I thought maybe talking to someone, anyone, would be better than these thoughts running dreary circles around my brain in a vicious cycle of self-defeat.

Many publishers waited until just before Sant Jordi to release their new titles, trying to feed the frenzy of book buying that would happen today and thereby launch these books with strong initial sales. That would hopefully turn into word-of-mouth recommendations as friends compared their Sant Jordi gifts over the next few days and weeks. It seemed as if all the books displayed by the first few booksellers were things I'd never seen before at stores, so I spent a while looking at the books and reading the back covers and flaps to see if anything tickled my fancy.

But as I made my way down the rows of booksellers, I realized that many stands repeated the same titles again and again. There were always variations, which made a quick stop at each stand worthwhile, for curiosity if nothing else.

Since I wasn't actively trying to buy a book for a lover, unlike everyone else here, it became almost like a memory game for me, of trying to spot as quickly as possible the few variant covers that I hadn't seen at the last table.

Ahead of me I saw a man who was obviously gay, with his close-cropped bleached hair and a dark goatee and an Ovlas tank-top that was the definitive clue hugging his gym-built torso, and a few seconds later he looked up at me as if aware of my gaze and our eyes locked in a complicitous moment. I don't usually try to pick up muscle-queens, so I wasn't really interested in following through and trying to talk to him or anything, but I felt gratified by our shared recognition of sexuality and possible sexual interest. That's something I so loved about how gay men cruised, it was so active, and so reaffirming, even if I was rejected or found the guy unattractive or whatever; especially right now it revived my ego to think that someone thought me cute enough to stop and look at me like that. Maybe I wasn't the only person here who didn't have a lover, I told myself, who knew what might happen? I thought that Muscleshirt was probably the type to live with his equally-muscled lover but they had threesomes with other gym queens or both still had sex outside the relationship. Tonight, however, they would give each other the books and roses they'd bought today, and no matter how often they fooled around with other guys they still had each other, too...

I walked away—from that table of books and from Muscleshirt—but the moment had changed my mood again. For a while, lost in the world of these books, I'd forgotten how alone I was. I began looking not just at the books that lay before me at each stand, but at my fellow browsers. I tried to imagine who each was trying to buy a book for, jealous of their relationship, and to imagine which few, like myself, were just here going through the motions. I wondered if I should pretend that I, too, was looking for that perfect gift to bring my lover. I sometimes felt as if I should buy a book—it didn't matter what—so that people didn't think I was a loser; it would be a sort of camouflage.

I tried to lose myself in the new books again, but now my eyes just glazed over as I stared at the descriptions of the plot or read the author's bios, so many of which mentioned the author's spouse and kids. To distract myself, I began to keep track in my head of which stacks of books were the most popular titles, and tried to find similarities between the men and women I saw buying them.

I got to the table run by the gay center Casal Lambda and stopped for a good look. A handsome man I'd seen a few tables up the Ramblas also came by and browsed, and didn't turn away when he realized that all the books on this table were gay or lesbian. I smiled to myself, as I watched him, and thought it hadn't just been wishful thinking a few tables back when I wondered if he were gay, too. He scanned the table, stopping to flip the occasional book over and glance at the back cover copy. When he reached the end of the table he looked up and saw me still smiling at him and he smiled back, then continued on down the Ramblas to the next stand. I walked over to where he'd been standing and put my hand on the book he'd last touched, wondering about him: who he was, what he was like, if he were single, if he were even really gay or was simply open-minded or maybe he had a gay friend he wanted to buy a book for...

I looked down at the book my hand was on, which was the new novel by Boris Izaguire, an openly gay television personality who was alternately loved and reviled among my friends (not to mention the gay press) for his queeny performances. Many criticized him for portraying the worst stereotypes of homosexuals and thereby selling out to the heterosexual image of us, while others saw him as a kind of camp icon who managed to break the invisible heterosexuals-only barrier of the world of television and make a name for himself. I was kind of indifferent; I found him entertaining when I saw him on Cronicas Marcianas, but I wasn't a fanatic about him (pro or con) the way some people I knew were. I hadn't read the novel yet, although I'd heard it was decent, and more literary than people expected from someone whose public persona was so... flighty.

I wondered how the handsome stranger felt about Boris, if he loved him or hated him. I looked down at the cover of the book I held, but saw instead the man's face again, that moment when he looked up at me and smiled. How I wanted to see him again, and especially, to make him smile like that again!

A couple of booksellers later, although on the opposite side of the Ramblas, I did see him again, my handsome stranger. I looked at him hungrily, as if I could devour with my eyes the sharp angles of his cheeks; I stared at how his fingers curled around the edges of the book in a way that bespoke of both gentleness and strength. He was holding the new Isabelle Allende novel, *Hija de la Fortuna*, and I wondered if he were considering it for himself or as a gift for someone—maybe even his lover. He put the book down and scanned the other titles on the table, before looking up and suddenly our eyes met and he smiled, his left eyebrow giving a little jump in recognition. He remembered me from the Casal Lambda table!

I smiled back and thought about him some more, wondering, wishing and hoping, entertaining fantasies of our building a life together. I know that it must seem kind of pathetic, to entertain such long-term fantasies about someone I had just met—or hadn't even met but had only glimpsed—but I did. I thought of us not just having sex together, though those images did cross my mind as well, but in a way that indicated that we were sharing a home together: maybe we were making love on the terrace of our apartment, or he'd be waiting for me when I came home from work, having missed me so intensely during the few hours we were separated that he couldn't wait to strip me from my clothes and tumble me to the floor until our bodies were joined as one creature gasping with pleasure.

I glanced away, embarrassed, as if he could read my mind from looking into my eyes, staring down at the book my hands were resting on and trying to think of nothing. When I looked up again he was gone, having wandered off to the next stand.

I stayed where I was, giving him a chance to move away and not think I was stalking him or anything. Although I couldn't help hoping our paths would cross again, perhaps a few stands down; I wondered if I'd manage to talk to him the next time we met. I was always shy when it came to picking someone up, even when I was interested—I was always certain I'd say something stupid and ruin any chance of our getting to know one another better. I hoped that if I put myself in range and stood close to him, he'd make the first move. Maybe I could make a comment about one of the books he was looking at, I thought, or ask for a recommendation... Yes, that would be best, since it would encourage him to respond, and once we began talking we might keep doing so.

At the Complices booth I saw him again, holding a copy of *El Ultimo Verano* by Paul Monette. He shifted the blue bellyband to read the text printed beneath it on the back cover, then put the book down. He picked up a copy of *Azul Petroleo*, the book by Boris Izaguirre I'd seen him look at early, and flipped it open to the first few pages. He stood there reading, and I hesitated going up to him right then, because it would be so obvious. My stomach felt like it had turned inside out and my hands got all sweaty. I stared at his back and wondered again where he stood in the spectrum of opinions about Boris, if he was a fan or maybe he was someone who hated him on TV and thus was curious about whether the book was any good or not.

I wondered if he had been considering the book for himself or not, and remembered seeing that Boris would be signing at the Antinous booth at 6:30pm. I glanced at my watch; it was 6:10pm. On an impulse, I decided to go back to the Antinous booth and buy a copy of *Azul Petroleo* for this stranger and have Boris sign it for him. It was a foolish impulse, I knew, but already my feet were bringing me back upstream to the Antinous booth; I guess it felt "safer" than going up to him and trying to start a conversation. At least now I would have a way to break the ice—by giving him the book—and I only hoped it wouldn't be too forward a gesture, that he'd at least understand. It was such an impetuous, romantic thing to do, it seemed right for Sant Jordi. But only a fellow romantic soul would recognize that.

Boris Izaguirre was animatedly talking with two middle-aged housewives as I patiently waited to have a book signed. Boris broke off mid-sentence and looked at me suddenly. "I just *Adore* the color of your shirt!" he exclaimed, clasping his hands together and giving a little jump. "Excuse me," he said to the two women, and moved slightly to be standing directly in front of me. He reached forward and took hold of the copy of his book that I'd been holding, waiting my turn. Meeting him in person, I began to see why the people who loved him loved him, he had a way of focusing his full attention on you, or at least making it feel like he was, and it made you feel like you were the most important person in the world to him right then, and that you were someone really special. It was an intoxicating sensation in a way, but it also left me feeling sort of breathless. It was like being under a spotlight that was too bright.

"Who's it for?" he asked me, his pen poised above the open book to write a dedication.

"I don't know," I answered, hating how high and weak my voice sounded because I was nervous. "I mean, I know who

I want to give it to," I continued, speaking too fast in a way that made everyone aware of my anxiety, I was sure, "but... I don't know his name. Not yet." I stopped talking, and finally dared look up at Boris, who was even taller and more imposing in person than I imagined from his TV image; most people were supposed to look smaller in real life, I thought.

Boris gave a little squeal of delight. "You're someone's Secret Admirer! How lucky this boy is! How romantic!" He wrote something in a fit of inspiration, and smiled again as he handed the book back to me.

Then Boris turned to the woman who stood to my right and said "Oh, I wish I had your hair!" She lifted one hand to touch the curls in question and blush, and as she did so Boris reached out for the copy of his book she held.

I felt relieved that his attention had moved on, while at the same time marveling at his ability to handle people so well, to so effortlessly shift from situation to situation with each new person, and make them feel like he'd given each of us a gift. But his intensity made me nervous, and I was glad to pay for the book and walk away before Boris looked at me again and realize how pathetic I was, that I had to resort to buying a Sant Jordi book for a stranger whose name I didn't know!

I bought a single long-stemmed rose from one of the flower stalls, and then hurried back down the Ramblas in search of my handsome stranger. We'd been steadily running into each other for so many stops now, I was sure he couldn't have gotten too far ahead of where I'd last seen him. But as I made my way through the crowd, scanning left and right for his blue sweater, for his finely-chiseled cheeks, for that smile that lit up his face when he'd looked at me... I began to feel nervous. Where could he be? Had I passed him and not realized it? No, I was certain I would recognize him, from any angle, if he was within my range of sight. But maybe someone had stood in front of him, blocking him from view... I wanted to run, to shout out his name—but, of course, I didn't know his name, not yet.

I reached the water without finding him, and then walked all the way back up the Ramblas, desperately searching for a sight of him again. But 15 minutes later I arrived back at Plaça de Catalunya and had to admit to myself that I'd lost track of him. What a fool I'd been, anyway, I told myself, to think that some stranger I'd exchanged smiles with would even want the stupid book I'd bought him. I was just a sentimental idiot!

I sat down on the curb, since the street was blocked off to cars all afternoon, and sulked. I felt like crying, as much at my own hopelessness as because the handsome stranger had gotten away. I stared at the flower I still held and thought it was such a waste to have bought it, to have even hoped.

I pulled one of its dark red petals and let it drop to the ground in front of me. "He loves me," I said aloud. I pulled another petal. "He loves me not." And then I was steadily stripping the rose, petal by petal, until only one petal remained, tightly curled in on itself, in the heart of the bud. I plucked it, and let it fall to the ground, and admitted my defeat. "He loves me not."

Why had I bothered with such a stupid game? I asked myself. More than ever I felt like crying, but I somehow couldn't, and I was torn between wanting that release of emotion, as if I the emptiness that welled inside me might drain away through my tears, and fear of appearing foolish to cry in public. I stared down at the pile of red petals that lay between my feet like a dark puddle. I felt like my blood had drained out of me and pooled on the street before me; that my heart lay there on the ground for anyone to step on. Angry—at myself, at my stranger for disappearing, at the world for not behaving the way I wanted it to—I stood up and stomped on the destroyed flower for good measure. It didn't change anything, but I felt a little better when I was done. At least I hadn't actually cried and embarrassed myself even further in public.

I wanted to throw the book from me, too, in its silver gift-wrapping, but I stopped myself. It wasn't right to take out my anger on the book, after all; it had done nothing wrong. Besides, I could always save it and give it to someone else—it wasn't signed to anyone in particular, just "To the Beautiful Stranger—How lucky you are to have such a handsome secret admirer! How romantic! I'm so envious! A big kiss, —Boris"

I thought of going to Sauna Casanova to distract myself, but it wasn't sex I was looking for. I was craving intimacy and romance; I wanted someone I could hold hands with and cuddle with more than I wanted a quick fuck from someone, no matter how sexy he was, who I would probably never see again, or worse, who I might run into again and have him not remember me.

I wanted to get as far away from there as possible. I thought of going down into the Metro, and just taking it anywhere. But instead I decided to walk up to Gracia, hoping the exercise might calm me down some, take the edge off this wild anger and frustration I now felt. I wanted to go someplace away from my usual haunts, and far away from the gay hangouts and bars. The last thing I needed right now was to throw my hopes at some other man, only to be rejected once again.

I reached Gracia far too soon, so I kept walking, even though I've always liked the neighborhood. It was once its own city, until it and Barcelona expanded so much they eventually grew together and filled the whole valley. But it still retained more of that feel of a small-town than most other areas of Barcelona, so I found it soothing.

I wandered north, not having a destination in mind, just trying to lose myself. It got dark, but I kept walking, thinking about my life, of the things I could be doing now, or my friends and how they must now be celebrating with their lovers and how alone that made me feel. It was a Friday night, but I didn't want to go out to the bars, and I didn't want to stay home. I certainly had enough things I could do, fixing up the apartment, stuff I'd been putting off during the week until I had more time. But to go home to my small apartment would just remind me that I had no one to share my life with, and I kept walking. For hours.

Eventually, I calmed down enough to realize I was hungry. I went into a corner bar and sat down at the counter, ordering a beer and a wedge of tortilla. When I was done I ordered another beer, and sat there drinking it and eating olives, not looking at anyone, trying not to think.

"It is you, isn't it?" a man said nearby. His face lit up in a smile when I looked up and saw it was my handsome stranger. "I mean, we saw each other earlier today."

"Yes," I said, hardly believing I had found him again—or he had found me, to be more correct—and here in the middle of nowhere. "At the Ramblas." One part of my brain was thinking: so that is what his voice sounds like, and filing the information away with all my other fantasies of him. It was a nice voice, warm and friendly, and I felt nervous because I knew I could get to like hearing it a lot. You'll only hurt yourself, if you think this way, I told myself, and tried to change my train of thought. But it was hard, with him standing so close to me again, and smiling that smile of his.

"What a coincidence," my stranger continued, as he stood next to me at the bar.

"Yes," I agreed. I didn't know what to say. I'm awful at making conversation like this, and I was afraid to seem too eager, and also too afraid to let myself hope again, only to later be plunged into an even deeper despair. My emotions still felt raw from having lost him at the Ramblas; I didn't trust that I might really have found him again, not like this, not by accident, not without cost.

"I was kind of hoping to run into you again," he said, and

I cautioned myself not to lose myself so fast again, to go slow and see what he had to say. "You see—I know this may sound strange, since I don't know you at all, but... Happy Sant Jordi." He handed me a bag, and I knew it had a book inside it. "I hope you like it," he said. "I had to guess what you might like, since... Well, since I don't know anything about you." He laughed nervously. "You must think I'm a freak, I know.

"No," I said, hardly able to believe what was happening. "I don't think you're a freak at all. I think you're just wonderful." I reached for the silver-wrapped package and handed it to him. "I bought you a book, too."

He looked at me mistrustingly, not believing I had truly bought it specifically for him, as if thinking I had this package set aside just in case something like this should happen, or that I was giving him a book meant for someone else. It was in that moment that I let myself hope again, that moment when he, too, felt uncertain and hesitant, that he was worried everything might suddenly fall apart.

"Open it," I said. "I saw you looking at it before. So I went and had him sign one for you. Even though I didn't know your name."

He was tearing away the silver gift wrap and his face lit up when he saw what the book was, but not nearly so much as it lit up when he looked at me and whispered "It's perfect. Thank you."

"It's signed," I said, and hated myself for it the moment the words had left my mouth. I sounded as if I were trying to convince him to like it, even when he had already said thank you, even when his face had already lit up. I hadn't even looked at the book he'd given me, which must seem so rude. But it was like I couldn't help myself, it's why I'm always so bad at making the first move, I felt so nervous I kept talking. "For you, I mean, although I didn't know what name to tell him."

"Julian," he said.

I repeated the name, seeing how it tasted on my lips, as he stared into my eyes.

And then a moment later we were leaning toward each other, our breaths and then our lips meeting, in a long wonderful kiss.

The Road to Love

I won't pretend I wasn't nervous as I walked out of the bus station in Badajoz and looked for Jorge. I was wondering if he'd really show up, if I were being a fool to come all this way on such short notice to see a man I hardly knew. Wasn't I too old for this sort of thing? I asked myself.

But then I saw Jorge's car and he began waving at me with this big grin on his face when he saw me notice him. I couldn't help but smile back, and I certainly didn't feel too old for this, I felt giddy as I crossed to where his little gray Volvo was double-parked as he waited for me. He leaned forward to open the door for me from the inside and I climbed in, tossing my daybag into the back. I was about to buckle my seat belt when Jorge stopped me. He pulled me toward him and we kissed, long and hard, our tongues probing deep into mouths as his hand ran along my left thigh, over my chest.

"Good to see you again," he said as he turned the key in the ignition and the car jumped to life.

"Likewise," I said, smiling uncontrollably, and I finished buckling myself in.

And Jorge pulled out onto the road and we were on our way

to Lisbon, taking advantage of the upcoming 4-day holiday "puente" for a little trip. Impetuous. That was the only word to describe this adventure. I stared over at Jorge, still feeling adolescently awkward but with a light feeling in my chest, and I wondered: is this going to be the one? I wasn't sure, but I was nervous, and that gave me a clue that I wanted him to be it, that this could work out to be a special relationship. It let me know that I was again ready to lose my heart to another man, and that I was liking this one more than I had many others I'd met in the past while.

Or maybe I was just tired, and getting older, and wanted the chasing, the searching, the yearning to be over with. I wasn't sure, but I had this little nervous feeling, and I felt good, really good. Either way, I was happy to follow this road and see where it went, even if it didn't go very far. It was too early to know how things would turn out. After all, I'd only known Jorge for two weeks.

As we drove along I thought of all the social rules of making polite conversation, that feeling that we had to always fill up the silence with chatter. I didn't feel Jorge and I needed that, but at the same time I wanted us to talk easily, and openly. And I had so many things I wanted to talk with him about. I wanted to learn more about him, about his family and his growing up, about his ambitions and dreams. We hardly knew each other. And I was tired, to some degree, of imagining, because there were too many possibilities. It was too infinite to wonder what his life was like and to wonder, too, if our lives were compatible, what compromises I would be asked to make for him—and which I'd in fact be willing to.

Jorge turned to look at me often, and each time it was like an electric charge went through me. But as good as it made me feel, it also made me nervous for our safety. He was the one driving, so he should be watching the road and the other cars, not me! But I was secretly glad that he kept turning to look at me.

Jorge was thirty-nine, only a few years younger than me, but I wasn't alone in thinking more than a decade separated our ages—in his favor. I think maybe it was his energy that made him seem so youthful to me, how I constantly felt I was lagging behind or struggling to keep up with him, no matter what we were doing, and that made me feel old. And at the same time, his vitality attracted me intensely.

I had met him purely by accident. It was a Saturday night at the disco Refugio, around 4 am. I was tired of dancing, and so walked off the dancefloor to stand against one of the pillars. When I looked up it turned out I had positioned myself squarely in front of where Jorge was dancing by himself, and when he saw me look up at him he smiled at me. That was the first time I felt that electric-like charge go through me because of one of his smiles. Then he looked away. But he kept looking back, and since I had nothing better to do I kept watching him, too, and eventually began moving again, just slowly, a little sort of shuffle to the beat of the music, and soon enough we had both moved toward each other and were dancing together.

I had been hoping for a rest, but Jorge's energy was infectious and it kept me going, even though I was so worn-out already. We were dancing, and then I realized we'd stopped dancing and were talking, standing very close to one another, and a little while later we were moving around again, playing to each other and then away, still in that tentative stage where we had definitely expressed interest in each other but nothing was set in stone, as it were: the night was still young, for all that it was after 5am, or maybe it just made us feel young.

I learned the basics about him: he was originally from Peru, had studied architecture in the United States, and had just moved to Málaga a month and a half ago to work on the project building the Picasso Museum there. He had come up to Madrid for the weekend, crashing on the couch of a friend of his.

The friend, Miguel, came over to talk to Jorge. I was introduced, and listened to his gossip even though I didn't know any of the people involved. I wondered how Jorge had met Miguel, if they had picked each other up on an earlier trip to Madrid and become friends, or perhaps they had known each other before he had moved to Spain. Possibly they met on the internet, these days it seemed the likeliest possibility. I didn't know, and the moment didn't feel right to ask, so I just smiled occasionally and moved around as if I were dancing in my own little world, giving them space to talk. But I was feeling nervous that something would happen, that Miguel would pull Jorge away to do something for him or with him or whatever and the moment we were having between us would be broken.

So I was glad when Miguel wandered off again, and Jorge's attention returned to me. He didn't try to explain any of it, he just picked up where we'd left off as if there'd been no interruption, and I let his energy carry me along.

A few days after I'd met Jorge, I was buying groceries in the basement of El Corte Inglés at Callao, and the man standing in front of me on the checkout line struck up a conversation with me. He was a Frenchman, visiting Madrid for a month on business. He paid for his purchases with a credit card, and after he'd signed the slip he held onto the pen and wrote his name and the number of the aparthotel where he was staying on the back of the receipt. Call me, he said, handing me the scrap of paper and staring into my eyes with unquestionable meaning. Because of his accent, and the way he stopped to think before speaking in Spanish, everything he said sounded like a pronouncement.

Why can't I meet someone interesting who lives in Madrid? I asked myself as I walked uphill toward Malasaña and my apartment.

I thought about the guys I had met recently. An artist from Barcelona I'd met the week before at the bar Lucas, who'd been in Madrid for a few days to deliver some paintings to his gallery. Then Jorge during the weekend, who I'd had such a good time with. And now this Frenchman, who I added to the list even though nothing had yet happened between us. Because he was still someone from elsewhere. Where were all the guys who lived in Madrid? Was it I who was not attracted to them, or was I too old for the fast-paced ultra-cool crowd here and only appealed to outsiders who didn't know better?

I couldn't decide if I was insecure, but not enough to pull off the attitude required to be ultra-cool, or if I was on the contrary too secure in myself that I refused to play such infantile games.

Whichever the case might be, I lasted all of three hours before calling Guillaume and making a date for the following afternoon.

I thought about Guillaume as I sat in this car with Jorge hurtling toward Portugal. I didn't regret our little tryst, or feel guilty about it at all. Jorge and I hardly knew each other, I reminded myself, and we certainly hadn't promised each other anything.

But my experience with Guillaume made me feel fairly certain that I was willing to promise something to Jorge, willing to give things a go, if that was what he wanted.

The contrast between the two experiences was enormous.

It wasn't just a question of sexual chemistry. Guillaume had simply wanted sex. Jorge, on the other hand, used sex to get to know me better. Sex was just one part—a very enjoyable part—of a larger communication.

During sex, we had talked sometimes, Jorge and I. There was no rush to the finish, even the first night we slept together. Usually, in a first encounter, one is so determined to "show off" and impress your trick with your sexual prowess. We would each cum more than once that night, but with Jorge everything was low key. We laughed, we made jokes. Sex was funny and it was fun.

Jorge traced a finger along the scar that ran from my hip nearly to my knee, and suddenly my past became part of our lovemaking. And once history had been brought to the encounter, it seemed to implicate that the future was likewise invited into bed. Even way back then at the beginning of it all.

The sex with Guillaume was fine. Perhaps if I hadn't met Jorge, I would've enjoyed it more—that sort of no-strings attached sex that exists in a purely physical world. But for mere friction, I could always masturbate—I was craving something more.

Over breakfast the morning after we met, Jorge distractedly caressed my arm or leg in public as we sat in the croissant shop in Plaza Iglesia San Ildefonso and argued over headlines from *El País*. It was a small gesture but an important one to me. It was a comfortingly possessive act, not at all limiting, but at the same time making a public declaration about his being linked to me on an intimate basis. It didn't really mean anything, in and of itself, I knew, but it might grow to mean something. If I was lucky. If we were both lucky.

Jorge talked easily as he drove. He told me about the drive from Málaga to Badajóz, and about life in the US and anecdotes about his coworkers and his former classmates. I wondered about his relationship with his friend Miguel, but

I didn't ask. I did not want to be possessive or limiting. And it didn't matter. Whatever relationship he'd had—or even currently had—didn't change the fact that he and I were developing a growing intimacy, which looked like it would be given the time needed to deepen.

I had just told him an ironic story about my brother-in-law, who works as a plumber, when I suddenly realized that we'd crossed over into Portugal when I wasn't paying attention. There'd been hardly any indication of a border, nothing physical like a river or a fence to demarcate where Spain ended and Portugal began. They just blended one into the other. Although everything seemed greener on this side. Or perhaps I was simply happy, and thus noticing the profusion of nature.

Is this what love is like when one is older? I asked myself. Not the flaming arrows of love at first sight of youth, but getting to know someone and then realizing you'd already crossed the border sometime back without realizing it.

"We're almost there," Jorge said, turning to look at me.

As ever, I felt that jolt of electricity and I smiled back at him, staring into his eyes. I didn't tell him to watch the road this time; he was already looking at it, the road of our future together. The road to love.

Märchen to a Different Beat

Hansel pulled a tootsie roll from his pocket and undid the wrapper as he watched his sister try to comb the knots from her long brown hair. He popped the dark chocolate in his mouth and threw the crumpled wrapper onto Gretel's vanity.

"I don't know how you manage to eat that stuff all day long and you're still thin as a rail," his sister said, watching him in the mirror as she struggled with her hair. "It's a miracle you still have any teeth left."

Hansel was always eating candy, always ravenously eating, even if he wasn't hungry. It was his way of coping with the way their stepmother had tried to get rid of them during the famine. Gretel had been bulimic for nearly two years after the incident, as if hoping she'd become so thin that no one would notice her again. For all that they were twins, they did have individual responses.

"Let me," Hansel said, taking the brush from her. "You're so nervous your hands are shaking." He pulled the comb gently through her hair, untangling the long silken strands.

"I do wish you'd come to the prom," Gretel said again,

for what must have been the fortieth time. "I'd certainly feel much calmer if you did." She smiled at him in the mirror, making sure he knew she was just teasing with this emotional blackmail, but also hoping it would work anyway.

"You know I don't want to go. I'd feel so left out if I went. Everyone would be there in couples except me, the homo, standing alone in the corner, watching everyone have the time of their lives." Gretel winced as the comb caught in a tangle and Hansel continued tugging too hard. "Sorry."

Gretel smiled genuinely at him in the mirror. "It's OK."

"Promise you'll tell me all about it when you get home? Especially about Scott. And I mean *EVERY*thing. You know what traditionally happens on Prom Night. Oh, he's so dreamy—I'm so jealous, if you weren't my twin sister I'd probably strangle you!"

The twins shared a laugh, and Gretel promised to tell him everything, yes, even about sex if they had any. They shared everything with each other, all their secrets—but then, for so many years, they were all each other had. They were so close that sometimes they could almost sense what the other was thinking or feeling, before it was vocalized. They were alike in so many different ways. They even had the same taste in men.

"Gretel!" Their father's voice drifted up the stairs to Gretel's bedroom, interrupting their thoughts and preparations. "He's here!"

"How do I look?" Gretel asked.

"Gorgeous," Hansel said. And it was true, she was stunning.

The doorbell rang.

"That's him," she said, looking frantically over the vanity's top for something, anything she might have forgotten.

"You've done everything already, don't worry. Just go and have a great time. And don't do anything you're not comfortable with. And tell me all about everything as soon as you get home! Wake me up if you have to!"

They could hear the murmur of voices in the front hall, their father's deep double bass and a higher tenor that was Gretel's date's.

"I'm so excited!" Gretel whispered, squeezing her brother's hand. "You can still change your mind about coming, you know?"

"You don't let up!" Hansel laughed. "Go and have fun with Mr. Handsome downstairs."

Gretel gave her brother a hug. "I'll miss you," she said, and then she hurried out of the room before he had a chance to reply.

Hansel stayed where he was, listening to her descend the stairs, the appreciative comments Scott paid her, the stern lecture from their father about responsible behavior. He so wanted to be in her shoes right now, to be out on a Big Date like this with a guy he was mad about. To have their conservative, undemonstrative father tell him and his boyfriend to have fun but not to stay out too late, and all his other standard worries and concerns about their general physical and moral well-being.

But then, Hansel had always been a sucker for stories about romance and chivalry and all that, and what better moment for it was there than tonight, Prom Night.

And what bigger torment for him than being gay? Even a girl who wasn't asked out tonight still had the hope, the dreams, the stories of generations of girls and boys who'd gone before her. But who ever heard about guys inviting other guys to the Prom, as Hansel so longed would happen to him? It seemed every story he'd ever read was about waiting for Prince Charming to come sweep him off his feet... Or at least, the girl off her feet. But that's who he sympathized with, the girl, waiting for Mr. Right to come along and—

"Hansel!" Their father's voice drifted up the stairs again, interrupting his musing. "I'm going over to the Parkers' to watch the game. Want to come along?"

His father was being kind to invite him, even though he knew that Hansel hated watching sports of any sort. "No, thanks, Dad!" Hansel shouted down.

"If you change your mind, you know where to find us."

"Roger and out," Hansel shouted back, just to let his father know that he'd heard.

Alone now in Gretel's empty bedroom, Hansel sat at the vanity where his sister had been moments before. He picked up the silver hand-mirror, one of the few objects that had belonged to their birth mother, who'd died when they were both young. His sister and he both looked alike enough that he could pass for her, he thought, with the right hair and clothes and such. He couldn't help thinking that, if they'd been born twin girls, he might be going to the prom tonight as well, instead of sitting at home, alone, feeling sorry for himself.

"Oh, I wish..." Hansel began, staring at his reflection in the small silver handmirror until tears blurred the image. The words caught in his throat.

Suddenly, coming from behind him there was a scurry of flashes of light, like a strobe light hitting a disco ball. Hansel blinked his eyes and stared behind him in the silver hand mirror. Standing behind him, somehow, was the tallest woman he'd ever seen, in a dress made of blue sequins that shimmered in the light from the vanity's row of tiny bulbs.

Hansel spun around on the vanity's chair. "Who?" he said, looking the stranger up and down. She was well over six foot, even without heels. "Who are you?"

"You might say I'm your fairy godmother. Or godfather. Or whatever." The stranger spoke with the deepest bass voice Hansel had ever heard. "I'm an old friend of your mother's. I gave her that mirror, in fact, many years back.... Anyway, why don't you just call me Mary. I'm your Mary Fairy." Mary flamboyantly threw her hands onto her hips and her elaborately painted lips pursed into a pucker, and Hansel realized suddenly that he was staring at a man in drag. Or a fairy in drag. Or whatever, as the stranger had said.

"A Fairy Godbeing," Hansel said, calmly. He'd faced the fantastic before, so it didn't faze him, not completely. "Why me?"

Mary sashayed over to the bed and sat down, crossing his legs firmly one over the other and smoothing the taffeta frills of his dress. "Oh, we've been keeping an eye on you two, ever since that episode with the witch and the house of candy. Speaking of candies, you wouldn't happen to have a breath mint on you?"

Hansel rummaged in his pockets and came up with a tin of Altoids.

"You *are* a darling," Mary said, taking two pills from the tin. His fingernails were at least an inch and a half long, and painted an iridescent shade of blue like the back of some tropical beetle.

Hansel closed the tin and then held it in his lap, unsure of what to say or do next.

Mary took the initiative. After all, that's what he was here for. "So you want to go to the prom?"

"Yes," Hansel said. "No. Oh, I don't know. I mean, I want to go, but I don't want to go there by myself. I don't want to go there and feel so alone, that there's no one else there like me. I mean, I know there are other gay men in the world, but... I want to meet someone my age. Someone who'll love me because of who I am, not because I'm young and cute and then toss me aside when they find someone younger or cuter. Someone who'll understand what it's like."

Hansel was shy about having suddenly been so revealing to a complete stranger, but he'd been desperate to talk to someone, someone who cared—and could maybe help. Mary said he'd been watching over me anyway, Hansel rationalized.

Just how much of his life had Mary watched, Hansel wondered; every moment since the candy house, or just occasionally? Did he watch even when Hansel went to the bathroom? When he was showering? When he masturbated?

Suddenly, his self-revelation was forgotten with newer worries.

"I'll be your date," Mary said, and the matter was decided. He looked at his charge's still-concerned face and placed Hansel's hand in his lap. "I may not be your age, but trust me," Mary said, his voice dropping a register, "I'm definitely male."

It had not been something Hansel had really doubted before, but he had now felt the proof in the pudding, as it were. For the first time. He was speechless.

"So, let's see what I have to work with. Stand up."

Hansel, slightly in shock, did as he was bidden.

"Turn around."

"Hmmm. It's a shame to hide your cute butt with such baggy pants."

Hansel blushed and wondered just how much Mary could see, and what he could see through, such as the baggy jeans. He began to feel that embarrassment he felt when naked in the lockerroom, and then realized it didn't matter—there was nothing he could do about it if Mary was indeed able to see through his clothes, as seemed to be the case. That knowledge, while intellectually reassuring, didn't make him stop blushing, however, as Mary looked him over frankly.

"OK, now let's see the shoes. It's part of the script, you know. What have you got available?"

They both stared down at his sad-looking Reebok sneakers, which had seen better days—years ago.

"Not a moment too soon," Mary said, his final judgment. He stood up, turning his back on Hansel, then walked over to the door of Gretel's closet and flung the doors open with a grand flourish. "Come over here," Mary said.

Hansel, still a bit awed by Mary's presence, and also a bit

cautious, remembering his last interactions with the supernatural, did as he was told.

"Now, stand in here for a moment," Mary said, fiddling with some of the many bracelets on his long forearms.

Hansel stood where he was and laughed. "I thought a gay Fairy Godmother would help me come out of the closet, not go into one."

"Very cute, darling. Now do you want to go to the prom and meet the man of your dreams or not?" Hansel nodded. "Then trust me and do as I ask you to, thank you."

Hansel stepped into the closet. His heart leapt into his stomach when Mary shut the doors on him, throwing him into complete darkness. Why had he trusted this outlandish, unheralded stranger, who could be as evil as the witch who'd trapped him in a cage and planned to roast and eat him once he was fattened up?

Because he desperately wanted to believe in what this Mary Fairy stood for, that there was hope for a boy like him who loved—or at least, wanted to love—other boys.

Suddenly Hansel felt a hand on him. He screamed, and tried to pull away. But there were hands everywhere, hundreds of them, it felt. He had no idea whose they were, or how they could even belong to any bodies, there were too many of them, all one atop the other atop his body. And, once his panic died down when he realized the hands weren't hurting him—and that there was nothing he could do to escape them—he realized that they felt rather pleasurable, rubbing themselves over every square inch of his flesh. He had a raging erection, he noticed, and felt embarrassed by it, wondering what would happen if Mary chose that exact moment to open the doors.

Which is, of course, what Mary did.

"Very nice," he said, staring down at Hansel, "if I do say so myself."

Hansel glanced down at himself, ready to cross his legs

and hide his hard-on with his hands. But it wasn't even visible beneath the dapper black tuxedo with a bright blue cummerbund that matched Mary's dress. He also wore a pair of shiny black dress shoes with a square clear crystal as each buckle; his glass slippers.

Speechless, Hansel crossed to his sister's vanity and stared at his new, ulta-chic image. He could hardly believe how sophisticated he looked, and a feeling of overwhelming insecurity gripped him. He reached into his pocket for a piece of candy, but his pockets were empty—not even lint!

"Nice, isn't it?" Mary said. "Now let's go show you off. Miss Thing doesn't have all night, you know. The prom only runs till midnight, remember."

"What happens at midnight?" Hansel asked, opening drawers in his sister's vanity. He remembered hearing stories of how fairy magic ran out at midnight.

Mary smiled. "Why, then the after-hours bars open, and the fun really starts. Come along, it's time for you to make an entrance." Mary swept out of the room in a cloud of taffeta and sequins.

At last Hansel found what he was looking for; a Hershey bar he'd tucked away as emergency rations. He had similar hiding spots all around the house for just such moments when his own supply ran out. He regretted not having eaten the gobstopper that had been in his jeans before his magical change of costume, but looking himself over in the mirror he couldn't argue that he was looking fine in these new threads.

As Hansel followed after Mary, he couldn't help wondering if his twin would recognize him when they showed up—not to mention everyone else. Was he making a horrible mistake?

"Hansel," the principal said, standing up from his chair

behind the table that blocked the gymnasium entrance. "We didn't expect to see you here."

Hansel looked away under the principal's bespectacled stare, forgetting that he had every right to be there, just like any graduating senior. He noticed the fancy clothes he wore, and knew that he cut a striking figure, no matter how small he felt inside. He stuck his hands inside his pockets, and suddenly felt the candy bar; suddenly he felt more reassured. He looked up again. "Well, here I am," he said, plainly. He smiled.

Mary put his arm around Hansel and squeezed his shoulder tightly.

"Yes," the principal continued, "here you are. With your lovely, um, companion."

Mary pursed his lips and kissed the air with a resounding SWAK!

"Well, then, do you have your tickets?" the principal asked, knowing very well that they did not. Hansel felt his back break out in a sudden cold sweat.

"We're on the guest list," Mary said, and began to walk past the principal into the auditorium, tugging Hansel with him.

"But we don't have a guest list!" the principal protested.

"You do now," Mary said, and turned his back on the man.

And sure enough, on the table before him was a clipboard with a sheet of paper on it that said GUEST LIST. There were only two names on it:

Mr. Hansel B. Gottsfried
Ms. Right To Mary

Inside the auditorium, his arm still around Hansel's shoulder, Mary whispered in Hansel's ear, "If you think a fairy gets upset when she's not invited to a christening, Honey, look out if you don't invite her to the prom!"

Hansel smiled, giddy with relief that they had pulled off their confrontation at the entrance. Already he was beginning to feel like this wouldn't turn out as bad as he had feared. People were noticing that he was there; Hansel imagined they might've been making bets earlier as to whether he would show, and who he would bring with him. They'd wondered if he'd bring a guy as his date, and he wondered what would've happened if he had.

And then Hansel realized that he had brought a man as his date, a man in drag, who looked as glamorous as any of the biological girls here. They were making a spectacle of themselves, perhaps, by their very presence here, but he was enjoying being the focus of people's attention. He was making them stand up and notice him, notice that he wasn't afraid of them, and wouldn't back down in the face of their fears or prejudices, the names they'd called him behind his back for all these years.

"I'll go get us some punch," Mary said, making a beeline for the beverage table. People moved out of his way, and not simply because he was such an imposing, tall figure.

Hansel scanned the room, looking for people he knew. Everyone looked so different in their formal wear, as if they were all royalty, princes and princesses for tonight at least. He saw a handsome man, and lingered on him for a moment, beginning to imagine fantasies of love and lust before he realized it was Scott, his sister's date. He was jealous for a moment, and then laughed at himself; he and Gretel were so alike in so many ways, even when it came to their sexual attraction.

Gretel, on seeing her brother, suddenly broke from her partner and came rushing over.

"Hansel! I'm so glad you're here. What made you change your mind?"

Mary appeared suddenly, handing him a drink of red liquid. "Here you are, sorry it took so long. They were serving Kool-Aid, can you believe? It took me a moment to stiffen it up. Hello there." Mary extended his arm, as if she expected it to be kissed.

"Gretel, this is...Mary. Mary, this is my sister Gretel, as you know, and her date, Scott."

"Sister, will you forgive me," Mary asked, handing Gretel his drink, "if I steal this handsome man from you for one dance?" She grabbed Scott before anyone had a chance to protest, or even speak, and led him out onto to the dancefloor. "I promise to be gentle," Mary called over his shoulder. Scott held Mary stiffly as they began to dance; he kept glancing down at Mary's crotch, as if trying to determine what lay beneath all those folds of taffeta lace.

"'As you know?' You have some explaining to do," Gretel said. She looked down at the cup she was suddenly holding, as if wondering where Mary's lips had been before drinking from it before her, then took a long drink from it anyway.

"Mary is my fairy godmother. Or godfather. Or whatever. He appeared out of nowhere, just after you left with Scott. Did the whole presto-change-o magic thing and before I knew it, here we are. Isn't he something?"

"You're not in love with him, are you?"

"With Mary?" Hansel scoffed. "No. He's hardly my type. But you must admit he is something else, eh?"

"That's for sure," Gretel remarked, somewhat sourly. But then she smiled. "But I'm so glad you changed your mind, and decided to come anyway. We'll have so much fun together!"

"Yes," Hansel agreed.

"Let's dance." Gretel dropped their cups on a bleacher and pulled her brother out onto the floor. They danced together for a while, enjoying the magic and glamour of the moment.

"Look over there," Hansel whispered to her. "It's Jack

Charming."

"Yumm," Gretel agreed, getting a quick glimpse of the boy they were discussing as the pair spun through the steps.

Jack had transferred in during the past semester, so hardly anyone knew him very well, though he was generally well-liked. He was very good looking, and he got straight A marks, and he'd been a star athlete at his previous school, though he chose not to compete at Henley High, taking phys ed. classes during the day. No one knew why he had switched schools so suddenly during his final senior semester.

"Why is he being a wallflower?" Hansel asked, as he and Gretel spun around. "I can't believe someone like him doesn't have a date for the Prom."

"Who knows?" Gretel said. Their movements had brought them next to Mary and Scott. "May we cut in?" Gretel asked, returning to her date's arms.

"Your sister found a keeper," Mary said, as he stepped into Hansel's arms. For a moment, Hansel wasn't sure whether he should lead or follow, since Mary was taller than him by a half foot at least, but after a moment's pause he stepped forward and took the lead.

"So are you enjoying yourself, Honey?" Mary asked.

"Yes," Hansel replied. And it was true. He was enjoying himself. He was jealous of his sister's boyfriend, he had to admit—to himself, even if he said nothing aloud. But he didn't really need to. That's why his Fairy Mary was here after all, to help him out in this special moment. As they danced together, Hansel wondered what it would be like to dance with a boy his own age who was equally in love with him, who would wrap him up in all the romance of this special night and not let go for years and years.

Suddenly, Hansel's reverie was interrupted by a deep voice that asked, "Can I cut in?"

Hansel felt his heart sink, wondering who wanted to dance with Mary. Couldn't they see that he was a man in drag? But then, Hansel hadn't recognized this fact at first. What would he do? He would feel so abandoned if he were left alone; everyone would stare at him, know he was gay and didn't belong here. He tightened his grip around Mary's waist. Please don't let go of me, he prayed silently to Mary, or I'll fall.

But Mary did let go.

And Jack took Hansel's hand and pulled him close. For a moment, they didn't know what to do, which should follow and which lead. They stood frozen like that for a moment, indecisive. Then Jack stepped forward, and Hansel stepped back, and though he wasn't used to following his feet seemed to know what to do. Perhaps it was Mary's magic, he thought quickly, before he thought only of Jack.

They danced together, and as the song ended, Hansel felt something hard pressing against his thigh. They stood close to one another in the break between music, and Hansel reached into his pocket. "Want to split a candy bar?" Hansel asked.

Suddenly he felt lame—he couldn't believe that *THOSE* were his first words to the man of his dreams! He should've said something flattering about Jack's eyes, or how hansdome he was, or any of a hundred thoughts that suddenly flooded Hansel's brain at once, now that it was too late.

Jack smiled. "I love Hershey's," he said. Hansel's face lit up with a smile, too, as he stared into Jack's blue eyes.

Across the room, Gretel noticed her brother and Jack had stopped dancing and moved off the dance floor. "I'm tired," Gretel told Scott, "let's rest." The moment she and Scott stopped, Mary was standing beside them, as if he'd materialized out of thin air. "Have you got anything left in one of those cups," Gretel asked, "I'm parched."

"Afraid not, Child," Mary said, turning both empty cups bottoms-up.

"Scott," Gretel asked sweetly, "could you please get us

something to drink?"

He glanced at Mary, as if somewhat nervous still to leave his girlfriend alone with him. Then smiled and went in search of drinks.

"So now that you've gotten us alone," Mary said.

"Is he going to be OK?"

"It looks like he's likely to have the night of his life."

"But it's not all some fairy glamour that's going to wear off at the stroke of midnight, is it?"

Mary looked wistfully at Hansel and Jack, who'd rejoined the twirl and surge of dancing bodies. "No, not this one. But I can't know what will come of this, no one can. There are many different ways of working magic, Child. Sometimes all it takes is giving someone a little self-confidence, and letting them take care of all the rest."

Gretel looked at her brother and Jack, who'd started dancing again, happily together. "I'm glad it wasn't magic."

"Me, too." Mary sighed deeply. He blotted at his eyes with a handkerchief that had appeared out of nowhere. "My mascara is going to run." Mary blew his nose noisily into the handkerchief, then looked up again at Hansel and Jack. "Ah, young love."

"Yeah," Gretel agreed. "It's so nice to see Hansel finding a happy ending at last."

"Child, we haven't even gotten to a happy ending yet."

"Oh? What'll that be?" Scott asked as he came up, handing them each a cup of punch

"You should see how big Jack's beanstalk can grow!"

Fag Hag

The witch's fork fell to the floor during dinner.
"Man coming," Avery told her.
The witch did not doubt her familiar. He had always been better than she at reading omens.
"I wonder what he wants," she said, wiping the fork against her skirt and knowing Avery would know. She stared at the cat, who would not open his yellow eyes to look at her. His tail swished back and forth over the edge of the table.
"Love potion. It fell facing East."
Instinctively, the witch looked to the window, where she could see the forest to the East of her cottage. She wondered if he would be coming from that direction, a traveler. Likely he would be just another townsperson from the South. She almost asked Avery, but held her tongue. The cat swished his tail and did not open his eyes.
After dinner, the witch carefully arranged her cottage while waiting for the stranger to arrive. Presentation was vital. She placed objects on the bricks of the hearth to cast shadows across the room. The phantom shapes flickered as the flames licked the wood, as if the shadows were alive.

"He's here," Avery said, not lifting his head from the table, where he lay on his back.

The witch cast a nervous glance about the cottage to make sure everything was in place. She hated surprises. She would have liked an extra few minutes to prepare herself for the encounter, but hurried to the door. Avery's hearing was far superior to her own, but soon even she could discern the footsteps on the path to her door. They stopped. The stranger paused, no doubt to steel his courage, and just as he raised his arm and was about to knock the witch flung open the door and cried, "Come in, come in. I've been expecting you." She turned away and left him to follow her into her intentionally-darkened abode. In her mind, she examined his image: she'd been expecting someone larger, she realized. No, not really larger, but older.

She turned to the boy who had come to her for help. "Now, for a love potion, you'll need to bring me some of her personal effects." He can't be more than fifteen summers, the witch thought. Younger than usually dared come to her for this sort of spell. "And they won't all be easy to come by, I warn you. I'll need a lock of her hair, which should be little problem to obtain. But I'll also need her blood, and not just any blood, but the blood from her menses. You'll have to find a way of getting some. It doesn't matter if its dried, if you can get ahold of her rags, so long as there's enough of it. There's just no making a love potion without it. And I'll need—" The witch stopped. The boy had not been looking at her, and he seemed... not exactly distraught, but something similar perhaps. She was used to people being fearful when they came to her, but this was different. "What *is* the matter?" she asked impatiently, for she had an image to maintain and she felt herself going soft around this boy for some reason. "You did come here for a love potion, did you not?" Could Avery have been wrong? she wondered. He was so good at reading omens, but there was a first time for everything.

"It's not for a girl," the boy said, quiet but firm.

The witch laughed. She tried so hard to intimidate her customers by knowing beforehand their desires. Their fear made them obedient and generous and kept her from worrying overmuch that she'd awaken one night to her cottage being burned by ignorant peasantfolk. But this time her assumptions had gotten the better of her.

"Can you still make me a potion?"

The boy was so earnest, the witch felt her heart going out to him. I'm definitely getting too old for this job, she thought to herself. Or perhaps she had simply been living alone for too many years.

"Yes, I can. It'll cost more, though, since I'll need to do extra research. I don't get much call for those, you understand."

The boy nodded. "I am willing to work for as long as is necessary to pay for it."

The witch regarded him again, and it almost took effort to not allow her surprise to show. Why did she keep underestimating him? He had no money, which should have been apparent. He was obviously a farmboy with that sundyed skin, despite his regal cornsilk hair and bright blue eyes. He was still young but already the muscles of his work showed on his light frame. She had bartered before, but usually with produce or livestock or objects, not labor. But she liked him, instinctively, and she was impressed with his courage and determination. It had been many years since she'd had an apprentice to help about the place.

"I'll expect you tomorrow at sundown, then, and every evening until I've decided you've paid the debt."

The boy looked at the witch for a long moment, not frightened, but not cocky, either. Judging, perhaps. At last, he nodded, and turned.

The witch smiled after he had gone. She imagined the

boy would grow less taciturn as he got to know her better. It would be nice, she thought, to have someone other than Avery to talk to.

"You're in a fine mood today," Avery complained.

The witch considered the cat's comment for a moment, and realized she was anxious about the boy's return. She bit back a retort to Avery and busied herself about the cottage, creating small messes for the boy to clean and repair.

"Why bother? There's work enough to be done as it is."

The witch ignored the cat, as the cat so often ignored her. She wanted the boy to start off on the right foot, without being lazy. She couldn't go about teaching him anything if he weren't willing to devote himself. And she also had an image to maintain; she didn't want him telling stories back in town about her personal life and effects.

"You understand," she told the boy, when he'd arrived at the cottage exactly at sunset, "that everything that goes on in this house is not to be spoken of—to anyone. Not your parents, not your friends. Not even," she said with a smile, "your prospective paramour." He turned scarlet, even his neck flushing low into his tunic.

She did not want to breed a too easy familiarity too soon, and thus teased him mercilessly, and was domineering. She tested him, measuring his capacity to think and to learn—and to obey. In dealing with magic, it would at times be vital that he follow her orders unquestioningly, despite the rational seeming of the situation, lest a spell go awry and destroy them both. Faith was often half the battle. Especially in the case of a love potion.

It was more simple to create the desired aphrodisiac than she had let on, but the witch had been so taken aback by the request, or rather by the inaccuracy of her assumptions, that she continued in her elaborate pretense and delayed giving the boy the potion, which she'd already completed, assigning him various quests to obtain hard-to-find materials she needed for other projects, or those which would throw him into contact with his intended love, to begin establishing a connection between them.

The boy performed each request without complaint. Every evening, just before sundown, he arrived at the cottage, presaged the first week by a warning comment from Avery, but soon even the cat came to accept his presence as unquestioned and the boy set to work on one task or another before the witch had noticed his presence. At last, she relented, and gave him the vial, though he was to continue working for her to pay off his debt for it.

She asked him questions often, about life in the village, and especially about his boyfriend. His replies were mostly a terse yes or no. Not out of fear of her, it seemed, but because he always spoke simply and directly, and chose not to speak at all when he did not have anything to say. His answers soon became more elaborate as the romance blossomed:

"He kissed me today."

"We held hands last night, when I left here, and sat talking beneath the elm at the crossroads and watched the stars."

But he never volunteered this information without first being asked. He seemed too shy, too bashful, even though the witch thought he felt comfortable around her and in the cottage. He was thoughtful and kind, and often took care of things she had not asked him to, simply because he had noticed they needed repair: bringing water from the river for her, mending the broken section of the fence that surrounded her cottage, transplanting the windowsill herbs.

The witch quite enjoyed his company, and the fact of having company about the cottage once again, but she stopped keeping him so late so that he would have time to spend with his love. That was, after all, the entire purpose behind his presence in her life, what he had come to her for. It seemed wrong, somehow, to deny it to him now, though she would be in her rights to exact such payment, should she so choose. The witch hardly regarded his presence about the cottage as payment any longer; he was, she realized with some alarm, a friend. She had not opened herself up, emotionally, to another person in so many years. She felt vulnerable.

The witch resolved to be merciless, to hold the boy at arm's length with taunts and work him as she would any apprentice. But when she tried she found that she could not do it, and instead listened eagerly to the boy's tale of last night's romancing. The two boys were now inseparable when not working, and very much in love, it seemed. The witch was quite pleased with her handiwork. And the boy was so happy she couldn't bear to shatter his joy and innocence by suddenly holding him at arm's length, and for no reason at all. She was intensely jealous each time the boy spoke of his blossoming love affair, but she was also happy for the boy, and took consolation in that. Definitely too old for this job, the witch told herself, as all her suppressed maternal feelings bubbled to the surface.

There comes a time when all mothers must push their young out of the nest. "You're welcome to continue to come to the cottage," she told him. "I am in fact eager for you to continue to do so. But if you come, it must be of your own free will. You have now long fulfilled your obligation for the potion."

The boy looked thoughtful, and the witch felt her stomach churn. She knew, in her heart, that he would now leave her, and though she had meant to set him free, she had never really expected him to fly away from her.

The boy spoke slowly and carefully, and managed to look at her the entire time. "Thank you for the offer. However, we will now be moving to the West, where my love has an estate that his father bequeathed him. We plan to live there, where we hope to be free of the prejudices we have found in town, where people do not acknowledge our love."

The witch felt betrayed. After all that she had done for him, grooming him to be her apprentice and learn the secrets of magic she could unlock for him, and he would leave her now. She was glad that she had not had children of her own flesh and blood. She imagined it must be even more painful when it was time for them to leave.

The witch felt herself pulling back into a tight emotional knot from which she resolved never again to leave. One must open oneself to the risk of pain in order to feel happiness, she knew—and she had been happier these past few months since he began coming to the cottage, happier than she had felt in many years—but it was hard to not instinctively lash out at the boy, for being, unwittingly, the cause of her pain. But when had this boy ever acted as she assumed he would? It was not his actions, but her assumptions which hurt her.

"Well, I'm glad to hear that my potion was so successful and that he is so very much in love with you."

The boy looked away and did not say anything.

"It would be appropriate to say thank you at this point."

"I... Um..."

"Whatever it is, you can tell me. You do know that, don't you?"

He gulped in a deep breath and said, "I never gave him the love potion, I dropped it before I had a chance to use it." He blushed, his neck and face turning red in his embarrassment.

A hundred thoughts and emotions crowded the witch's mind and heart. She ignored them, and tried to think rationally. "If you didn't use the potion, then why did you come work for me all this time?"

"You had performed your half of the bargain, and I felt it was only fair that I uphold my end of our arrangement, even though I did not, through my own fault, get to use what I had bought."

"And you never told me that he fell in love with you on his own!"

"You never asked. And I didn't know how to tell you without angering you, since you'd said it was so difficult to prepare the potion and I'd wasted it. You'd always assumed he fell in love with me because of your potion, and it was easiest not to correct you." He looked at the floor for a moment, then back up at the witch. "But in a way, I'm glad," he said at last. "That I didn't use the potion, I mean. This way, he fell in love with me because of who I am. He wasn't coerced into it by a magic spell. I know that he truly loves me."

The witch was insane with jealousy, constantly comparing this boy's success to her own aborted love affairs; no matter what happened, everything fell into place for him.

No, not everything. They would face prejudice and hate and misunderstanding for the rest of their lives, similar prejudices to those she had experienced as a witch, being feared and misunderstood. None of her lovers had understood or trusted her, and she had never allowed herself to earn their trust. This pair seemed perfectly suited to each other, and she was glad that they had found each other to cling to, to face the rest of the world,

"Very well, then," she told the boy, letting him go because she knew she must. "You must follow your own destiny. I would ask one request of you, though: I would like to meet him, before you go." Meet this boy who is stealing you away from me, she left unsaid. She forced a smile, and the boy smiled back at her and nodded, and in that moment the witch knew that there had never been room in this boy's heart for anyone but his love, certainly not an old witch who had chased away everyone she had ever loved.

Season's Greetings

It had been a long time since I could remember snow in November, but it was hardly unheard of for New York City. The weather had been so wonky the past few years, with global warming and El Niño and whatever new causes or theories they were blaming now, that I wasn't really surprised by anything that fell from the sky any more, no matter the season.

I was surprised, however, as I checked my mailbox while waiting for the elevator, to discover I'd gotten my first Christmas card of the year. I know that traditionally the Christmas sales season starts the day after Thanksgiving and all that, but this was way too early for a card. I briefly contemplated waiting a few weeks before opening it, when Christmas felt like it was in high gear, but I've never been good about delayed gratification; even when I was younger, I'd sneak into the living room when no one was looking and pick up my presents under the tree and shake them to try to determine what was inside, even though I knew I'd be in big trouble if I opened them before Christmas day itself. I could, however, wait until I'd gotten upstairs and had warmed up a bit, before opening the card; after all, I knew from the postmark that it was from John.

I stomped my waterproof boots on the mat outside my apartment door, and took them off so I didn't track snow inside. I took off my hat and gloves and scarf and jacket and one of the sweaters I was wearing, and put a pot of water on to boil for tea. I looked at the AIDS benefit calendar hanging on the fridge, with black and white photos of naked men by Jeff Palmer, and confirmed that it was indeed still the 29th of November—far too early to be getting Christmas cards.

I took the pile of mail and sat down on the cushioned window seat I'd built over the radiator and hence suffused with a delicious warmth. There was a catalog from J. Crew, a bill from AT&T, and two different envelopes filled with coupons from local establishments. I opened both of the latter and rifled through the traditional storage and car service adverts, looking for the coupon for my local grocery store and anything new that caught my eye.

Then I opened John's Christmas card. It depicted a foil-embossed wreath and had a preprinted greeting inside that read: WITH ALL WARMEST WISHES FOR JOY THIS HOLIDAY SEASON. John had printed my name and signed his own above and below the store-bought sentiment. That was it.

I didn't quite understand why people bothered to send cards that said so little. Two bucks for the card, $.33 cents for the stamp... to say absolutely nothing, except maybe "remember I'm alive." Passive-aggressive blah blah blah.

John was a guy I'd tricked with three years ago in Montana on a business trip held in one of those convention centers so far off the beaten path the rates were dirt cheap, so all sorts of miserly industries liked to hold their trade shows there. John was the stereotypical blond farmboy type, big and beefy and dumb as a post. The sex had been delicious in that purely physical way sex can be, when two bodies are equally aroused by each other and fit together as if by magic. He had one of those cocks that bent kind of funny even when it was hard, and I was sure it would be awkward to find a comfortable position for him to fuck me as a result; but maybe I know less about the insides of my rectum than I thought, since no matter what we tried (and we tried many variations that night) felt great.

John was tender and sweet and affectionate, even if we had absolutely nothing in common to talk about when we were not fucking. I'd given him my address in New York so he could look me up if he ever came for a visit, more than willing to spend another night of blissed out pleasure with him if the opportunity arose. I couldn't fathom spending time with him with any regularity. And I hardly wanted to maintain a long-distance affair with him—they're taxing and difficult in the best of circumstances. But I'd be happy to see him again for a fuck.

I tossed John's card onto the pile of junkmail and wondered if he'd ever come to New York. He obviously still remembered me enough to send me a Christmas greeting, empty though that greeting had been. I thought about his cock and the way it had felt in my mouth as I held it there, waiting for it to get hard for a third time that night...

I unbuttoned my jeans and pulled out my dick, thinking about John and the sex we'd had. It didn't take long for me to have a full erection. I remembered again the funny bend in John's dick as I stroked my own, and tried for a moment to twist my cock into that same bent shape. It didn't quite work, and I quickly gave up and settled in to my usual masturbation stroke, pulling long and hard along the shaft and stopping sometimes near the glans to rub the sensitive skin on the underside just below the crown.

I glanced out the window at the thick white flakes of snow falling from the sky and noticed that my neighbor across the street was watching me jerk off. And not simply watching, he had his dick out as well and was jerking off in time to my own motions.

It's a bit of a shock to suddenly discover you are having sex with someone else, when you didn't realize you weren't alone. And even though we weren't having what would traditionally be called sex, that's what it felt like nonetheless, sex with each other even from our separate apartments across an alleyway slowly filling with snow.

I wasn't sure what to do, so I didn't do anything. That is, I kept jerking off, and he kept jerking off, and we watched each other. He had a nice body, from what I could see of it through the storm and the distance. He was completely naked, whereas I was still clothed with just my crotch exposed. I paused in my jerking off to take off my other sweater and unbutton my shirt, leaving it on my shoulders but open.

My neighbor was very different from John's beefy bulk, which I had just been fantasizing about. My neighbor was sleekly muscled, with nice definition on his abs and especially his obliques. He was that olive complexion that could be from any of various Mediterranean or Middle Eastern cultures, and had dark hair and dark eyes and a matt of black hair across his chest but not all the way down his stomach.

I tried to think if I would stop to cruise him if we met on the street, or if this were one of those types of encounters like in a bath house, when you're horny, and you engage in sex with the most attractive of what's available and often have a perfectly enjoyable time even though you might not, ordinarily, have thought to pick up that given man, had you run into him on the street with all his clothes on. Sometimes, in a steam room, attributes which are not obvious in the "polite" world of social gestures and clothes prove to be quite enticing when encountered by the hand, the eye distracted by clouds of vapor or dim light.

I couldn't decide. I was a little nonplused by the suddenness of it, my being unaware of his being sexual with me before I had had a chance to decide if I wanted to be mutually sexual with him, but it was more surprise than any sense of violation or distaste. Of course, that may simply have been because I thought he passed some ill-defined mark of handsomeness, or because I was horny from my fantasies about John and from not having had sex or jerking off in a few days.

I watched the way his arm flexed as he tugged on his dick, which curved gently upward in the classic erection. My own dick was more direct, sticking straight out from my crotch at a perpendicular angle. I shifted so I was kneeling on the window seat, and pressed my dick up against the window pane so it stood upright, so my new friend could see it better. The glass was cold, making me clench my balls involuntarily and flexing the muscle at the base of my dick, thrusting it harder against the glass.

The whistle on the tea kettle went off, but I ignored it. There were five cups of water in it; it would be a while before it boiled itself dry.

A bead of pre-cum ooozed out of my dick, white like a little puddle of melting snow. I pumped my ass muscles, rubbing my dick against the glass and making a little trail across the pane as my neighbor's arm moved faster in its motion. I wondered if anyone else was watching, and what they would think, but I didn't really care, caught up in the moment of our sex. I sat back onto my heels, still facing my neighbor across the alley, and took my dick up in my hand again. His hand and cock were a blur as he jerked off with the intent to cum, and I too began to move my arm faster, squeezing with my fingers as my hand slid along the shaft and cupping my balls with my other hand, to help with the race to the finish. I felt, for a moment, like a teenager in one of those infamous circle-jerks I had never had the luck to take part in when I was actually that young. Of course, I was born too late to play games like "sticky biscuit" where everyone ejaculated onto a cracker and whoever shot last had to eat the soggy mess. I smiled wryly to myself at the ironic thought that this was almost a metaphor for what safer sex had come to, during the epidemic: two men jerking off with each other from across an alleyway. But actually, I felt we had more intimacy, despite the physical separation, than some of the men I'd tricked with here in the Big Apple.

My neighbor leaned forward suddenly, his breath fogging the glass in front of his face so I could no longer see his features clearly. And then suddenly there was a second smaller shadow lower down, a series of white splotches that together made a sort of Rorschach blot image of a dove before they began to drip toward the floor.

He waited for me even after he'd cum, a gesture I found touching, especially considering the anonymity and distance inherent in our encounter. He lingered in his window, running one hand through the splotches of his cum as if he were using his semen to make a finger painting for me—or caressing my body from afar, using the window as a substitute for my skin, a metonymy of sorts. I squeezed my balls tight with one hand, clenching that muscle that makes them pull up higher against my body, and pumped my hand faster, wanting to cum for my neighbor. And after a short while I did, my hips bucking forward as I ejaculated, although I kept my back arched so that I sprayed lines of semen across my own chest instead of the window pane or the fabric of the cushions.

He smiled as I came, his whole face lighting up, and once I had caught my breath, I smiled back at him. Then he disappeared from his window—presumably to clean up. I ran my fingers through the viscous clumps of cum that clung to the clipped hairs of my abdomen or slid down toward my crotch, thinking I should do the same. I stood, cupping one hand to catch the runnel of semen so it didn't fall to the floor, using my other to hold my shirt away from my sticky chest as I went into the kitchen. I turned off the stove, then wiped myself off with a paper towel, rearranging my clothes as I finished.

Mug of Red Zinger tea in hand, I started walking back to the living room. Through the doorway, my warm, comfy window seat beckoned, and I thought about my newfound neighbor. "How very interesting," I said aloud before pausing and lifting the mug to my lips. I smiled and, still standing in the doorway between rooms looking out toward the window beyond, took a sip of tea.

I didn't see my neighbor again for days.

At first, I was constantly aware of his possible presence any time I was in the living room, that he might, at that moment, be glancing across from his apartment—or perhaps he was even actively waiting to catch a glimpse of me, as I sometimes did, idly passing in front of the window as if to check the weather and looking out toward his apartment. I thought of him especially whenever I sat in my window seat, as I did often in those cold days that grew shorter and nights that grew longer. But if he sometimes saw me, I didn't ever catch sight of him, our schedules off-sync except for that one brief moment of, yes, sex, the intimacy we had shared across the gulf—both the physical chasm between our buildings and the emotional anonymity that cloaks New York City—that separated us.

I was intrigued by him, and not simply because he was sexy and relatively convenient. It was so uncommon for someone to acknowledge the voyeurism we all practiced. New York being an island, we build upward since we can't expand out to the sides. Buildings are crammed up against each other, and, naturally, we can see into the apartments of our neighbors sometimes, but it is one of the unspoken rules of New York that you never acknowledge this—otherwise, how could you live in comfort, constantly aware of your neighbors' surveillance? As I had been, since our encounter—although in this case, I was not perturbed by it, and was in fact eager for it to happen again.

The unusual snowfall melted by the beginning of December, and walking home through the streets crowded with Christmas shoppers, I would sometimes pass a handsome man who looked back over his shoulder at me, and we would both stop and turn around on the pretense of window shopping and start talking. I always tried to arrange for us to go back to the other man's apartment for sex, feeling somewhat self-conscious because of my neighbor, certain that even though I didn't ever see him, he must be as obsessed with my private life as I was with the idea of his. I thought my neighbor might be jealous to see me with another man, and then I realized that his jealousy might be a way of my luring him to the window again.

The next man I met who made my dick leap to attention at the thought of what we might do together I invited back to my apartment and undressed him in the living room, sucking his dick from the window seat. But I was too distracted to enjoy his body, thinking about my neighbor across the alley who did not appear, and soon I moved us into the bedroom so I could focus on the quite-enjoyable sex with the man at hand and not the idea of possible sex with the one I was obsessed with.

The next time I saw my mysterious neighbor was on December 11th. I didn't get home until late because of the office Christmas party. I was sitting in the window seat reading the day's mail, as was my habit, when I realized I had a Christmas card from someone whose surname and address I didn't recognize. It was here in the city, and was addressed to me, but I had no idea who it was from. The card was a winterscape image of ice skaters with SEASON'S GREETINGS printed on the inside. It was signed Grant. I looked at the envelope again for the surname, trying to remember who Grant Hopkinson was, when a photograph I hadn't noticed previously fell out of the envelope and at last I recognized who it was from.

The photograph was a naked shot of a guy I had tricked with a few months ago, in an amateur porno-style pose where he's grabbing his dick low to make it look bigger. I hadn't given him my address, but as we'd had sex at my apartment after meeting in some bar (probably Splash), he must've taken note of the building and apartment numbers and my last name on his way out. We hadn't exchanged phone numbers to see each other again, but he'd written his phone number on the back of his photograph, I guess in case I changed my mind and wanted to have another round of sex with him. The photo wasn't bad, and from what I remembered the sex had been fun enough, but I figured he must be a lunatic, and the whole manner of his trying to reconnect like this, in a Christmas card, without even a real note attached, turned me off to the idea of seeing him again.

I tossed the card aside but kept the photo. I unbuttoned my pants and pulled out my dick, working it until I had an erection. I grabbed my dick low along the shaft and tried to mimic the porno pose of Grant's photo. What is it that makes us so desperate sometimes to be seen as pornographic? I wondered. Is it a genuine desire to be an exhibitionist or do we rather crave to be desired by as many men as possible and seek to achieve that aim through exhibitionism? I looked out the window and thought about my neighbor I hadn't seen for so long now. What he and I had shared across our alleyway was a private moment between the two of us, even though any of our neighbors could very well have been watching us from their windows—uninvited participants in the spectacle of our intimacy.

He was there again now, watching me as I aped Grant's photo. I smiled at him, waving my dick at him in exaggerated fashion. He waved his back. His pants were already tugged down around his knees, although he still had on a flannel shirt. His dick poked out from between the two flaps of fabric, like the lever of a slot machine. I wanted to tug on that lever again and again like an addicted gambler until I won the prize. But I was too far away to even reach the handle, in much the same way that the jackpot always eluded the gambler, the dream, the aspiration that kept him coming back because he couldn't have it.

But in a way, I already "had" my mysterious neighbor, possessed him, even though we had never touched, never kissed, never felt our bodies pressed deep inside each other. I pulled long and hard on my cock, watching him, enjoying that we both were jerking off expressly for each other, that we had this curious connection from across the divide that separated us. Only in New York, I thought—although I imagined it was possible that these sorts of encounters did occur in other places. But what was transpiring between us, this relationship, was something that seemed to define the wacky nature of life in New York, a city where these sorts of interactions were more-or-less commonplace.

I came first this time, spurts of cum splashing against the window pane and falling onto the cushion. I'd wash it later, I thought briefly, flexing my arm again and again to milk the last drops from my dick, not wanting to stop for anything. I kept my eyes on my neighbor as I came, smiling back at me; I felt I had his undivided attention, he wasn't thinking about what to make for dinner later or whether he had paid the electricity bill yet. He was just watching my body, the sex we were having from across our separate buildings, and enjoying the sensations of his own masturbation playing out what he could only fantasize about from across the split.

When my body stopped trembling, I leaned forward and kissed the window, making a pucker print against the glass. I watched my neighbor, who was still jerking off, but I was in no rush for him to cum quickly. I was half afraid that if he did, I would never see him again—even though he lived next door to me. That, too, was something so New York; there were people who lived on my own floor who I'd never seen in the three years I'd lived here. I studied his body, the way he moved, the way he jerked off. He leaned forward and let his tongue hang down, wagging it as if he were trying to lick his own dick. I wanted to lick it too. He let a glob of spit fall from his lips, catching it right on the head of his dick and then using it to lubricate his fist.

He came quickly with the lubrication, and I filed that little datum for future reference, as I continued to watch him. He brought his fingers to his lips, licking the cum from them and sucking on his index finger as if it were a cock. As if it were my cock, his eyes locked with mine. Then he grabbed his dick again and waved it at me, a farewell, before disappearing into the far recesses of the room.

I lingered in the window staring out across the alleyway, enjoying the warmth of the radiator below me and the afterglow of orgasm, thinking about these two encounters with my neighbor and wondering how soon it would be before I received my next Christmas card.

My mailbox remained empty of cards for many days on end, and I began to feel nervous—although the truth is I didn't usually get that many cards. I'm a bah-humbug sort of guy and used to think of them only as a nuisance, those obligatory cards from clients and all, but now I was desperate for them. Time was trickling by quickly—soon Christmas day itself would be upon us—and what if I never saw my window buddy again after Christmas had passed? We seemed to have this magical connections only if I had a Christmas card from some past lover or trick. I looked at the row of cards I had placed in the window around the window seat; they formed a sort of advent calendar, marking off the days/encounters we had had together.

I took some comfort in the fact that I had not yet sent my own cards, and I hoped there were others like me, who waited until the last minute, whose cards would arrive after Christmas day itself. I also hoped that there might be cards that were *en route* but were delayed by the sudden general increase in mail volume.

What would happen when I stopped getting Christmas cards altogether, though? Would we ever again connect? What would happen if we met on the street? Would there still be the same sexual tension between us in person? Or was there some extra glamour that came from being connected across such a distance, like the emotional safety of jerking off to a picture of your boss in the privacy of your home, fantasizing about him in a way that when you were in front of him in person you couldn't imagine ever realizing, because he seemed so unappealing in the flesh.

On the afternoon of Christmas Eve I came home to find a card in my mailbox at last. It had no return address, so I didn't know who it was from, but that hardly mattered. My dick leapt to attention as I stood in the hallway in front of the mailboxes, contemplating what should transpire when I went upstairs and opened it. My libido was well trained now to produce this Pavlovian response.

I distractedly waited for the elevator, having to make pleasant small chat with the Irish mother of three who lives two floors below me, who kept going on about how excited she was that her brother had come to visit for Christmas and other inanities. Alone at last in the elevator after the 4th floor, I breathed a sigh of relief and leaned against the fake wood-paneled wall, squeezing my crotch with one hand and adjusting myself within my pants. The card was addressed to me as Mr. Bowes and the postmark was from within the city; I had no clue as to who it could be from.

I dumped everything on the couch as I came in and hurried over to the window seat, tearing open the envelope as I went.

The card showed a naked hunk, with a Santa's hat over his crotch. I opened it. It was a blank card, in that there was no pre-printed greeting, just a hand-written note from the sender, which read:

> *Hi, my name is Robert. I live across the alley from you. I looked your last name up on the buzzer, guessing which apartment was yours. I hope I guessed right! I like what happens when you get a card. If you want to let that happen with me, give me a call sometime.*

He'd signed the card with his phone number.

I ran one hand over the hard bulge in my crotch and looked up. In the window across the alley was my neighbor, Robert, watching me and smiling. I smiled back, put his card on the window sill, then got up to look for the phone.

The Story of Eau

Our kitchen table is a once-elegant claw-foot porcelain bathtub nearly as old as the building, with an inch-and-a-half-thick slab of oak laid on top of it. The tub is wonderfully deep; in my last apartment, up in Hell's Kitchen, I had a normal tub: which is to say, both too short and too shallow. While my current tub in the East Village apartment I share with my lover, Tim, is still on the short side for someone like myself who stands on the far side of six feet, it compensates by being deep enough that my knees don't stick out into the cool air when I sit in it, as they have in almost all my previous tubs. It was perfect for sitting in for long stretches of time, relaxing and reading—provided one wasn't fussy about maybe getting the pages wet. But ever since my doctor ordered me to take two or three sitz baths each day to cure my hemorrhoids, I've had better things to do in the tub than read.

You might not think that getting hemorrhoids could improve the sex life of a balding thirtysomething-year-old gay man living in Manhattan, but then you don't know my lover, Tim. (If you're one of his ex-lovers, then you're lucky enough to know what I mean. But I'm the luckiest of all, since I'm the one who has him now. Knock on wood.)

In order to encourage me to follow doctor's orders and take all of the prescribed daily baths, Tim has taken it upon himself to create a little bathing ritual to pamper me. I tease him sometimes that his tender ministrations are really motivated by self-interest, since the sooner I'm healed, the sooner it'll be that he can fuck me again. But I have a feeling that even after I'm well, we'll continue our little bathing rituals (although probably not two or three times per day!)

We used to take baths only rarely, and not just because the bathtub was in the kitchen and also used as our dining table, which meant it was always covered in stuff, from dirty dishes to piles of bills. Admittedly, it required a concerted effort to decide to take a bath, since one had to first clean off the kitchen table, then remove the heavy table top. But even the effort and time-lag of running the bathwater took far too long and was too much trouble for the pace of life in New York City, let alone the extra hassle. It was a luxury we never seemed to have time for, or didn't often allow ourselves to take even when we did have the time. We had a shower in a tiny closet, and a toilet in a closet of its own right next to it, both of which also stood in the large kitchen that the apartment's front door opened into. East Village apartments are like that, sort of hobbled together after the fact, instead of having been designed to be a living space. But they were cheaper than just about anywhere else in New York City, and necessity made a lot of things worth putting up with.

Our little bathing rituals developed because one of the first times I took one of my post-doctor's-visit baths, Tim was home watching me. You'd think that after all the trouble of running a bath, I'd sit in it for a while. But I felt foolish, especially when I thought about why I was doing what I was doing and thinking it would never really work. Of course, negative thinking is the worst thing one can do in one of these alternative therapies, but that's what I was thinking, and that sort of thinking is what made me stand up after about four minutes.

Tim would have none of that, though. "Where do you think you're going?" he asked me. "I'm done with my bath," I said lamely. "Not yet, you're not," Tim said, "now sit down," and I did, as he disappeared into the bedroom. He came back a moment later with something behind his back. He stood behind me and I leaned my head back against the rim of the tub to look up at him. He smiled down at me and ran one hand along my torso and neck, leaning forward so he could kiss me. His other hand was still behind his back and I wondered what he held there, but then I closed my eyes and thought only of our tongues and our mouths until we paused to each catch our breath. I let my arms dangle over the sides, my head resting against the lip of the tub, my eyes still closed as I soaked in the warm water, and I thought "this is nice" and felt my body suddenly lose its tenseness, everything opening up, even my anus, which felt almost like a fist unclosing, with that sense of relief you feel after you let go of anger.

It was at that moment that I learned what Tim had been holding behind his back—handcuffs, which clicked around my wrist and one clawed foot. "You fink!" I cried at Tim, although I didn't open my eyes. I didn't want to move from the warm place I was in, both the bath and the afterglow of our kiss, which had kickstarted my arousal. Maybe that was part of the warmth, I thought, the flush of blood rushing through my body to fill my cock. With my eyes still shut, I felt the cold metal loop around my wrist and said to Tim, "I want another kiss."

He didn't answer, but a moment later I felt his presence behind me again, his body close, and then his fingers were touching my chest and neck, caressing my throat as they moved to float lightly over my lips. His breath followed next, warm and fragrant of the vanilla-pear tea he'd been drinking after dinner, his lips hesitating a hair's breadth away from mine. My tongue poked out to lick at him real quick and I said "Ribbit" and we both laughed. And then we were breathing the same breath again, our mouths sealed tightly to one another as he held my chin in his hands and our tongues tried to wrap themselves around each other. One of the first things that made me fall in love with Tim is how well he kisses, how it makes you feel there's nothing in the world he wants to do in that moment except kiss you, that he hasn't another thought in his head. So many men I've kissed not only lack the talent or the natural advantage of Tim's thick pliant lips, but you can tell their mind's not in it—they're worrying about whether they left the oven on or what bills need to be paid before next week or whether your kiss will turn out to be the beginning of an ongoing romance or a one-night stand or perhaps just a kiss. Tim's kisses could make me forget the worst of days at work and think only of him and our romance, and his agile tongue sent waves of sexual energy coursing through me.

"I thought I was supposed to relax," I complained when we broke apart and I'd caught my breath. I lifted my hips so that my erection poked out of the tub like the periscope of a surfacing submarine, its blind eye looking at Tim.

I waited for his reaction, wondering if he would just leave me like this. I was at his mercy, after all; even aside from the bath, I was still cuffed to the tub, with the keys still in the bedroom, for all I knew.

Tim smiled and dipped a hand into the warm water to slide up and down my inner thighs. I relaxed my hips and sunk back to the bottom of the tub. Tim's fingers kept stroking and poking along my legs and crotch and balls, before dropping down to hover near my tender asshole. "You're supposed to relax here," he said gently, his poking fingers as soft in their touch as the tone of his voice. His other hand plunged into the water and grabbed my cock as he said, "But that doesn't mean we can't get a little excited elsewhere."

My entire body tensed. He just held my cock in his fist, as his first hand poked at my asshole again. "Relax," he commanded, and I let my breath go and tried to follow his command, again imagining my asshole opening like an unclenching fist. "Much better," Tim said and started gently stroking my cock with his other hand. The motion created small waves that made my balls bounce; it felt like warm mouths sucking at all the skin of my groin at once.

"Much better," I agreed, closing my eyes again as I leaned back and purred while one of Tim's hands moved on my cock and the other gently probed my ass. I could feel a bead of precum building and I squeezed once to send it shooting out, wondering whether it would float to the surface or just sit at the tip of my cock.

Tim's hands stopped moving. "What?" I asked, opening my eyes.

He explained, "If you don't stay relaxed here" and his fingers swirled along the crack between my cheeks for emphasis, "I stop moving here," and again his fingers danced for emphasis, this time swirling around the underside of the crown where he knew I was most sensitive. My back arched instinctively as his fingers rubbed along there, and I knew I was starting to clench my asshole again, but I stopped myself, breathed out, and focused on keeping my asshole as open as possible. The pleasure in my cock kept building as his hand swirled around the glans.

"That's my boy," Tim said, and after a moment more he let me relax, sliding his hand down onto the shaft and beginning to pump, the change in stroke allowing me to catch my breath and adjust to the new, differently pleasurable sensation. Tim knew my body well, and knew how to work me, turning me on until I was about to crest over into orgasm and then changing his grip to delay things, over and over again, until at last I couldn't hold back any longer.

"I'm going to cum," I warned him. "I'm going to clench, and don't you dare stop!"

Tim didn't stop and a few seconds later my hips were bucking as I came, my dick spewing above the rippling water like a whale's blowhole spray.

My orgasm had splashed water all over the place. I looked over at Tim, who stood by the tub, his shirt and pants clinging to him. With my free hand, I reached across myself and started rubbing his hard cock where its outline showed through the wet fabric of his pants. I hooked my fingers behind his belt buckle and pulled him toward me, since my reach wasn't very good given the awkward position I was in.

"I think my bath is done for tonight, don't you agree?" I said, tugging on my anchored arm until the cuffs clanked against the porcelain tub. "I think this'll feel much better for both of us if you let me loose again."

Tim looked down at me with a gleam in his eye as if he were thinking of leaving me chained there for good. My fingers squeezed his cock tight, and then I let go of him, settling back in the tub as if I were completely unaware of his presence. Tim hesitated a moment longer, looking down at me in the tub as I tried my best not to look up at him or crack up laughing, before he headed into the bedroom without a word. He let me stew a good while, wondering if he planned to spring me after all, whether he'd gone to bed, if he'd lost the key. But eventually he returned, sans his wet clothes, but with the key to the handcuffs.

His cock had begun to soften from the state it had been in under his wet clothes, but it was still half-hard. It throbbed slightly as the blood pumped through it as he stood beside the tub. He held the key up and my eyes shifted from his genitals to his hands. "You want out," he began, making his dick give a jump as he flexed that muscle in the perineum that I was supposed to be relaxing, calling my attention to his crotch again. I didn't need any further encouragement and eagerly opened my mouth to earn my release—and his.

And thus began the bathing rituals.

The rituals vary, depending on the time of day. Night-time baths are more elaborate, which isn't any great surprise since both of us have more time then and less pressures from the world outside our little apartment. But there are certain other intrinsic factors that lend themselves to this sort of extra elaboration at night, like lighting. By day, there's really not much you can do, one way or the other, to create a mood or atmosphere with lighting, but for our nightly baths, Tim has bought these enormous three-wick scented candles which he'll place on the windowsill or the stovetop or the floor. They cast a soft, flickering light and perfume the air with their aromatic essences—vanilla, lavender, jasmine—all of which help cast a quiet, romantic overtone to what we're about to enact, the perfect ambiance in which to relax into each other's love and caring and our mutual desire. Sometimes, when Tim is feeling playful, he'll make shadow animals with his hands and cast them against the far wall, the porcelain's tub, my flesh beneath the water's ripples. His favorite is to cast a wolf's head and have it stalk across my body until the image snaps at my cock beneath the water. Depending on Tim's mood, the Shadow Wolf either tries to bite it off or perform fellatio.

If we're eating at home, the night ritual starts with dinner. But even if we're dining out, our repast plays a healthy part in the healing, since I've had to cut back on certain foods that can irritate the hemorrhoids. Thai is pretty much verboten for now, since all my favorite foods are either spicy or have nuts, and Indian and Korean have likewise proven too rough on my sensitive system. Also forbidden is my after-work Snickers bar while waiting for the subway. One of the advantages of living in New York City is that we've got every type of cuisine from around the world, so there are still plenty of savory options I'm allowed. Most of the time we eat at home anyway, not just because it saves money but because both Tim and I love to cook.

It doesn't matter whether Tim or I am preparing dinner, it's all part of the ritual. We're beyond the score-keeping stage of the relationship and simply relish in the nourishment of feeding and our pleasure in eating—and the other pleasures that are to come.

Sometimes, while we're cooking, Tim will slide the tabletop a few inches and begin running a bath. The wood lid serves to keep the water hot, and as we eat, the tub radiates warmth to our legs. It's a delicious feeling that starts the relaxation as tension begins to drain from our legs and drip away through the soles of the feet. Because New York is such a pedestrian town, we're all of us on our feet all day long, dealing with the hassles of commuting and crowds and worrying about being late and in general just pounding the pavement.

And once the food starts to hit the stomach, satisfying both hunger and taste buds, it's so much easier to let go of all that stored-up tension and worry from the day. Which is what made the rituals as important as the baths themselves; they removed, or at least dealt with, some of the possible causes of the hemorrhoids in the first place. They were an attention to the details of daily pleasures in our lives, all those small sensory moments of joy that we so often overlook or don't consider significant. And the most important part of the rituals, the togetherness, is the truest panacea that exists.

All of those small details, more than the sex we had before, during, or after I slid into the warm water, was what came to matter most to us. Sex was just one of the ways we expressed our delight in each other, that giving of pleasure and the receiving of it in return.

Mind you, we like the sex a lot too, wet and messy as it often becomes. Night-time baths always begin slow and gentle, with Tim and I taking turns using a sponge across each other's bodies. We've bought water toys for each other: rubber duckies and funny soaps and wind-up plastic frogs that kick their legs and swim. I bought a little catnip mouse the day after Tim bought me a small boat, and we played Stuart Little for a while until our playing with each other knocked the mouse and boat out of the tub. Sometimes Tim would join me in the tub, sometimes he'd stand outside it, naked by my side. Either way, we'd usually wind up splashing water all over the linoleum by the time we were done for the night and moved into the bedroom to drift into sleep or the living room for some mindless television viewing while we cuddled.

The daytime baths have their rituals as well, although neither of us can really afford to take as much time with them because of our jobs. But the whole act of this enforced daily relaxation has made both of us aware of how much daily stress we had in our life, from jobs to socializing to just getting through the day, and how much of it was self-imposed. Taking time out to interrupt our hectic schedules has been proof positive that we can stop to smell the roses, as it were, and calm down and still accomplish everything important that we need to.

Often, when we are on tight schedules at work and can't afford to run over time, Tim will come home on his lunch break a half hour before me. He'll cook something for us to eat and begin to draw a bath for me. By the time I get home, he has eaten already. I am ordered right into the tub, and it is only when Tim has to head back to work that I'm allowed to get up and dry off and get dressed again. I am also permitted to eat whatever Tim had cooked up for me.

It was hard, sometimes, to relax for these lunch-time trysts, when we always had to keep one eye on the clock. But at the same time, it was invigorating. There was something both romantic and illicit about having a "nooner"—quick sex in the afternoon before going back to work—and I think both of us tackled our afternoon's tasks with more pep as a result.

For day-time baths, Tim didn't fill the tub entirely. I'd already showered in the morning, and the important part of my anatomy, as far as these baths were concerned, was my ass; with only a few inches of water in the tub, my sore ass was sure to stay covered.

Of course, before any bathing—night or day—there is the undressing. No matter how pressured we were to get back to work, undressing me was one thing Tim never rushed. Often, during the day, I was not allowed to undress Tim in turn, since we didn't have the time for sex or we had to be careful to keep him from getting wet. Sometimes I'd unzip his fly despite his protests, and suck his cock while I soaked my rear. We didn't always climax during these daytime baths, that wasn't the point. And Tim never seemed to tire of making me feel like he truly cared that I was healing, that he was an active part of the cure. I'm sure that if anything helped me get better, his love was the medicine that did it as much as the baths, that focus and attention he paid my body as he slowly pulled a sock from my foot, holding my leg with his other hand to support it as the sock came free, and lowering my leg gently back to the ground until I could put weight on it and support myself again.

At night, we had the time to peel each other from our clothes, and it was like pulling away all the cares and worries of the outside world, until only the two of us remained, stripped down to the essence of our being and our relationship, our skin raw with desire for one another. And we kiss and embrace and caress one another, and our movements send candle-lit shadows flickering, and whirls of steam rise from the porcelain claw-foot tub in our kitchen.

And to think that when I was a kid, I used to live in terror of one of my parents saying those two most-feared words, "Bath Time!" Oh, what a world of difference being in love makes!

Occasion a Need

Between classes I trudged through the snow to the post office. The city plows had created huge, nigh-impenetrable buttresses to the sidewalks, like the snow forts I had built as a child with my next door neighbor and best friend, Stevie. Some frosh were making snow angels in front of Yale Station and I watched them for a moment, staring at the marks they left behind like large, alien hieroglyphs—or perhaps I thought that only because I had just gotten a C+ for my anthropology paper on Mayan Calendric Runic Inscriptions and hieroglyphs were still on my mind.

ACT UP had set up a table in front of the banks of mailboxes and some volunteers were giving out condoms. I'd only come out last semester, though I'd been furtively having sex for years, but ACT UP still made me nervous. I guess I'm not used to confrontation, to being so militant, even though I know I ought to be. Especially now. They're fighting for me, and I'm afraid of them.

Jimmy stood up when he saw me and walked forward. "Happy Valentines Day, Peter."

V-Day. I'd forgotten.

"I haven't slept with anyone in over four months," I said, refusing the proffered silver-foil packet. "Not since... You know."

"I know. And it's a shame. You're cute, and I know tons of guys who'd like to sleep with you, even knowing you're sero-positive. Get a grip, Peter, it doesn't mean your sex-life is over."

We'd had this argument before. "Yeah, well." I walked past him and down the row of boxes. I knew, intellectually, that sex could still exist for me, but I just couldn't get my mind to conceive of my actually doing it, not when sleeping with me could mean someone else's death.

I had two pre-approved credit card offers and an overdue notice from the library for a book on Mayan hieroglyphs I'd checked out for my anthro paper and never read. Maybe I'd have gotten a better grade if I had. The book was propping up the couch in the living room, where I'd been sleeping for the past two weeks because my roommate Robert had a new boyfriend.

"Just take it, Pete, you never know what will happen. Possession will occasion a need."

I took the silver square, if only to get Jimmy off my back.

"Atta boy. You can at least stick it into your journal, if you don't find any better uses for it."

There was a thought. Jimmy and I were both taking an art history course called AIDS And Its Representations. We were supposed to be keeping a stream-of-consciousness log about our thoughts on any reference to HIV or AIDS in the media or our lives. I was the only one in class who was actually positive—at least, so far as we all knew.

I put the condom and the letter from the library into my backpack, pulled the hood up on my jacket, and braved the icy New Haven winds as I made my way across Old Campus to my English class.

❧❧❧

I sat on the couch (a.k.a. my bed this week) and tried to concentrate on my Rocks-for-Jocks problem set but all I could think about were Robert and his boyfriend fucking in the bedroom, getting *their* rocks off. Much wasn't left to my imagination; the dorm walls were so thin I could hear every caress, let alone Robert's screaming, "Yeah, Brad, fuck me hard!" every other minute.

I rummaged through my backpack, looking for something less demanding to better occupy my attention and came across my mail. I unfolded the library notice and the condom Jimmy had given me in the post office fell into my lap. V-day. Shit. I'd forgotten for a happy while.

I stood up and pulled the hieroglyphs book from under the couch, which listed heavily. I tried various other books, and combinations of books, but nothing else fit quite right. I had to sleep there, after all, and couldn't be rocking back and forth all night, so I put the Mayans back under the couch and decided to just pay a late fee. Or rather, to have Robert and/or his boyfriend pay the late fee, since they were directly responsible for my not returning the book.

I picked up the condom again, wondering exactly how long it had been since I used one, remembering the one time I hadn't. I was tempted to walk into the bedroom and give it to Robert and Brad, but instead I pulled out my AIDS And Its Representations journal, paper-clipped the condom to a blank page and wrote a long entry about the post office, V-Day, and listening to Robert and Brad fucking. I was still writing when my train of thought was broken by Brad crying "I'm gonna cum!" and I realized I had a hard-on from listening to them. I felt sick. I had to get out of there. I grabbed my coat and ran out into the snow as I put it on. Everything was white, the whole campus blanketed in white, pure snow. I walked aimlessly, kicking at the drifts, not wanting to go home, not really going anywhere either until I remembered there'd be a movie tonight at the Med School. The film society there showed movies every Thursday for two bucks. I hiked up the hill, only to discover tonight's feature was the ultra-romantic *A Room with a View*. V-Day. I'd forgotten. Again. I almost turned around and walked home, except I could still hear Robert and Brad's muffled grunting in my head and I bought myself a ticket. I swear, I was the only one there alone.

I needed to get away for the weekend, away from Robert and Brad and my homework and everything else, so I went to New York to visit my friend Michael at Columbia. While the train waited at the platform in New Haven (it was delayed by the snows) I stared out the window at a poster for *Angels in America*, and kept thinking I really ought to see it someday, considering how everyone raved about it, and also how it would now have a very personal meaning for me. I dug my AIDS journal out of my knapsack and began to write about the presence that show has had in my life, even never having gone to see it.

A cute blond sat directly across from me. I smiled back at him, but nervously buried my head in my notebook again and hoped he wouldn't talk to me. Was he trying to pick me up? He kept watching me intently. He was cute, but I wasn't in any mood to talk right now.

He dug a notebook of his own out of his bags and we both sat there, furtively sneaking glances at each other and scribbling away. After we hit Stamford, when the train ran express to Penn Station, he interrupted me, and showed me his notebook. It was a sketchpad, and he'd drawn a picture of me. I was naked, with a hugely disproportionate erection. Totally unrealistic, but I was finding myself turned on by my own picture! And also by the fact that that was how he saw me.

I didn't know what to say to him. I looked him over, appraisingly, finally giving him serious consideration as a fellow sexual creature. I liked what I saw; I'd known that from the moment he'd sat down across from me, but was I willing to...?

"The train doesn't make any more stops until New York," he said, standing up and walking towards the lavatory.

How long do you plan on staying celibate? I asked myself. All you have to do is be safe. He's cute. Go for it.

I could feel my stomach tying itself in knots as I stood up and put my journal in my bag, but not before taking the condom I'd paperclipped to one of the pages and dropping it in my pocket as I followed him into the bathroom.

There was a swagger to my steps as I walked through Penn Station. I was certain everyone could tell I'd just had sex for the first time in months. I felt great!

So maybe Jimmy had been correct, I thought, as I took the subway up to 110th street. Possession will occasion a need. And once I had awakened that need, it wasn't about to disappear. Suddenly, every man was a potential sexual partner. I hadn't felt this randy since I first discovered ejaculation!

I stopped at a drugstore before going to Michael's dorm, and bought myself a box of condoms. Trojans, although I would've preferred Ramses. However, they were the only kind the store had, and I didn't want to go hunting all over the city on account of a brand name! Jimmy's voice kept echoing through my mind like a mantra: possession will occasion a need will occasion a need a need a need.

I stopped at a cafe for coffee to warm up, and pulled out my journal to write about that boy on the train. I worried a little about what my professor would think, since the account was so explicit, but I didn't really care right then, I was still riding high. It was not talking about sex which made so many people have unsafe sex in the first place, so I spared no details. If nothing else, I thought, my prof should find some titillation when it came time to grade my journal! I wondered if there was something similar I could do to help my Mayan Archeology grade...

Since I'd written extensively about the condom I'd paperclipped to one of the pages, expecting never to use it, never to be having sex again, I took one of the new condoms I'd bought and paperclipped it into my journal. I was a new person, I felt, as I poured my psyche and libido onto the page, after all those months of being afraid to have sex, of remembering that one time I had sex without a condom. Sex was an integral part of life, even for someone HIV-positive, and I wasn't about to pretend any longer that it wasn't.

The waiter kept coming over to pour more coffee into my cup or more water into my glass or to ask if I wanted anything more. I knew what he wanted and wanted him to know I knew, so I left the page with the condom open on the table as I stared up at him, smiling. We kept flirting like this for another fifteen minutes, never saying a word other than the coffee-shop small talk, until at last he sat down at my table with me.

"I see you travel ready for everything," he said, staring directly at me with rich, coffee-black eyes and meaning, of course, the condom which lay between us.

"Indeed," I said, knowing I'd be writing about him in my journal soon.

Jimmy was drawing pictures of naked men in his notebook. I didn't know if he was feeling bored or horny; I felt both right then. Professor Sternberg was handing back our AIDS journals. I might've drawn pictures of naked men myself, except my palms were so sweaty as I wondered how he'd reacted to the level of sex in my journal that I couldn't hold a pen.

Suddenly, my journal was in front of me on the table. There was an A+ written across the front.

"I very much enjoyed your journal," Professor Sternberg said, before handing out the other notebooks.

I was in shock, but eventually I became simply smug. I flipped open my journal to see if he'd made any comments about any of the sections. I was especially curious to see what he'd said about the explicit sections. I'd practically filled the entire journal with sex episodes, at least after that condom Jimmy had so innocently given me on V-day.

I flipped back a few pages and stared at the mint-flavored condom that was paper-clipped into the journal. I'd left a Trojan.

I laughed out loud. He'd enjoyed my journal all right!

I turned to Jimmy and said, "Possession will occasion a need."

He smiled and asked, "What are you doing after class?"

WATER TAXI

The rough orange fabric of the life preserver was rubbing my nipples raw. It was times like this that I was glad I hadn't let Jaume talk me into getting my nipple pierced when he had his done. I liked the way it looked, the small silver loop, especially since he'd only had one side pierced; I don't know, when men have both sides done it makes me think of door knockers, and the whole aesthetic changes and loses something. But I thought he must be even worse off than I was right now, since the pierced tit was supposed to be even more sensitive than before, and no doubt the life preserver was scrunching and twisting the piercing with each shift of movement.

Jaume, though, didn't seem about to complain from what I could see. He sat at the prow of the kayak, his powerful arms dipping to one side and then the other as he paddled. His shoulders were hidden under the life preserver, but I could watch the musculature of his back flex as he twisted left and right with each stroke, and I wondered once again what I'd done to be so lucky to have such a beautiful man as my boyfriend. I felt lucky about everything right then—Jaume, the crystal clear blue sky, the afternoon sun, the warm surf, the party on the beach, life in general. I forgot about my sore nipples and matched Jaume's strokes and we just glided across the waves for a while.

We'd neither of us used a kayak before, and thus when the DJ announced free kayaks as part of this year's Gay Pride Festival on the beach, Jaume and I had jumped up from our beach towels and trotted over to the launch area. This was the first year that Barcelona had a Gay Pride Festival held at the beach, with an afternoon full of activities like volleyball games and speakers blaring dance music and the like. Later in the evening, we'd all move into the Pabellon del Mar behind us for a long night of dancing and performances by bands like Baccara and Folkloricas Arrepentidas and drag shows by Arroba and other queens I'd never heard of. And of course, normal club dance music in between all that. It was expected that many men would come just for the dance. Half the money from the entrance would go to the fight against AIDS, so there was a revindicative side to the festivities as well.

I wondered if it would work. The gay political groups of Barcelona were always fighting, one with the other, and this year they'd split off, with one group having a gay pride march on June 28th, commemorating the Stonewall Revolution back in the US that was the start of the modern homosexual rights movement, and with the other half, including most of the owners of the gay businesses, deciding to hold a more festive event on Sunday, July 4th, to try and get a better turnout. It was Independence Day in the States, they joked, and they were breaking free of the US domination of gay culture in other parts of the world. After all, they said, why should we celebrate an American Gay Pride Holiday instead of creating one of our own?

I sometimes feel guilty that I'm not more politically active, but the truth of the matter is, I'm easily bored by such things. I know it's important to vote, and I do, but I just can't stand the endless squabbling at meetings and arguments over which subgroup of the organizations feel they're not getting enough representation and so on. I mean, I'm glad there are dedicated activists out there who understand the legal jargon better than I and know how to play the system and who're fighting for my right to kiss my boyfriend on the beach like I'd done a few minutes ago. Like many of the guys out here on the beach today, I'm sure, Jaume and I were just here to have fun. We'd gone to the march on Monday to show our support and help boost the numbers—now that the groups were split up we figured it'd be especially important to put in an appearance—and we'd also come to the fun-in-the-sun party.

My mind was wandering as my body worked through the simple repetitive task of our kayaking, but I was woken from these musings by a call from a pleasure boat that had drawn up anchor in front of the beach, neither especially near to nor all that far out from the shore, as if undecided whether they wanted to simply watch the festivities or be included themselves. Apart from the all-male crew aboard the deck, it was obvious from even a quick cursory glance at their postures as they stood about drinking afternoon cocktails and watching the shore, that they were not here by mistake and had come for the Gay Pride party.

One of the men, blond and shirtless, was leaning over the side and hailing to us. I was sure it was us because when he saw us glance up he waved in our direction, but I glanced over my shoulder anyway. I had that feeling like when you're in a crowded bar and a guy you think is cute smiles at you, and you can't believe he's really smiling at you, certain that one of his friends or some hot number must be standing just behind your shoulder and is in fact the intended recipient of the smile.

"What do you think?" Jaume asked, not breaking his

stroke. We were angling parallel to the beach, and if their boat had been in motion our paths would've crossed in a hundred meters or so.

"Why not see what he wants?" I answered, using my oar to change our course. "Maybe they want to buy us a drink?" I laughed and our little kayak spun around toward the boat, and in a moment I again matched Jaume's even strokes.

As we drew up to the boat, the shirtless blond moved to stand at the deck's ladder. It turns out he was dressed in a skimpy pair of bright orange speedos. "Can you take me to shore?" he asked. "The water's full of jellyfish."

I looked him over, and from the angle we were at I got a good look at certain parts. Which, I had to admit, looked quite good from this angle.

Jaume and I have been together for nearly two years, during which time we've tried a number of different relationship options, from complete monogamy to a period where we were hardly having sex with each we were each slutting around so much, which led to our having a trial separation and eventually coming back together for our current agreement: whenever we wanted something outside our relationship, we would do it together. Which doesn't mean that we always wound up in threesomes, although that was usually the case. Sometimes we would go to a sauna together, and maybe each of us pick up someone; the cabinas weren't really big enough for all four of us to go into one and have our two separate pairings, but the one time we tried it was pretty exciting, watching Jaume get fucked by someone else while he watched me fuck the trick I'd picked up. I still felt some jealousy, but at the same time I felt Jaume was including me in his pleasure and he in mine.

But most of the time, we were happiest with the more-traditional threesome, and our taste was similar enough that we usually didn't have too many disagreements—at least among ourselves. It was not always the easiest thing convincing our prospective third, but actually many guys have a fantasy about doing threesomes, and they're not always so easy to come by in the typical bar or dance club scenario (as opposed to, say, a sauna, where they're easier to arrange) so many men were willing to give it a shot when we asked them. I always think they took one look at Jaume and decided they'd put up with sharing him for a chance at sex with him, half a cake being better than no cake. I'm just glad I'm a deciding voice in who I share him with.

Since both Jaume and I have active libidos, we're usually always up for anything attractive the other proposes. So I boldly asked our blond boatman, "And what's our fee for the taxi service?" while rubbing my crotch with one hand in an unmistakable gesture. Jaume, looking over his shoulder at me, glanced down into my lap and smiled, his silent agreement to what I'd proposed, then looked up at the guy on the deck as we waited for an answer. He looked down at the bulge growing in my skimpy blue swimtrunks, glanced out at the shore for a moment, then back at Jaume and me.

"OK," he nodded, "come on up," and he stepped away from the side of the boat.

I, too, looked back at the shore, my mind crowding with thoughts: I wondered what people could see from the beach. I wondered if anyone would see us board the boat and especially if the kayak crew would get mad at us for getting out of the kayak. I wondered if our stuff, still on the beach, was safe, or if someone had run off with it. I wondered if it was perhaps unwise to climb onto a boat full of strange men; what if they were the proverbial axe-murders, who dumped the body bits overboard where the fishes ate up the evidence? I wondered what our prospective passenger looked like without his bathing suit, and I nudged Jaume in the back with my oar. "Let's go," I said.

We tied the kayak to the bottom rung of the ladder and then climbed up it, taking the oars with us. After all, the last thing we needed would be for a wave to knock them into the water while we were up on the boat, leaving us all stranded out here. Besides, I figured if we had them with us, it'd be less simple for one of the guys on the boat to steal the kayak while we were off it; I was still feeling a little suspicious. But I'd always been cautious; even with tricks on land, I was wary if I brought them home, making sure there were no easily-pocketed valuables lying about and guarding my wallet someplace unexpected. I'd never had any problems, but it didn't hurt to be on the safe side, I thought.

I followed Jaume onto the deck and found we were surrounded by a group of maybe seven men—some in swimsuits, like we were, others in more ordinary summer clothes. They were all eyeing us, as if they were feeling suspicious, too. And who could blame them? Or was there something more than curiosity in their gaze? How much of our interchange had they overheard? I wondered. And what did they think of it, those who'd heard and understood?

The guy who wanted a ride stood with the rest of them, but he didn't really blend into the crowd. Maybe it was because he was the only one I recognized—he had an identity separate from that of the group because I'd first seen him alone, leaning over the side of the boat as he called out to us. Also, he stood a step apart from them physically, as if to underscore the fact that he was leaving, and they would stay. As I took in the other men, who were as varied a lot of homosexual types as one could imagine, from an overdressed highly-coifed queen to a quiet butch number who looked like an ultra-straight soccer player, I wondered if he'd always been part of this mixed crew or if he'd swum out here. I glanced at his crotch, but his swimsuit was dry. But all that meant was that he'd been onboard long enough to dry out. I thought, as I watched, that his basket gave a small jump, as if in anticipation of what we planned, and I smiled, as much at the thought of our imminent sex as the idea of how

I imagined this was making him feel. I glanced at the other men as I idly rubbed my crotch, but got no sexual connection from any of them. Suddenly, I wondered less why he wanted to go ashore while the rest of them stayed aboard.

Our blond made no move to introduce us or himself, and I wondered if we were planning to do whatever it was we would do there in front of everyone. It would hardly be the first time we had an audience, so it didn't really phase me, and I was sure it wouldn't be much of a problem for Jaume either. I reached over and helped him unbuckle the life preserver, letting it fall to the deck. It made a small clatter as the buckles hit the wood, and the noise seemed startling loud in the absence of any social chatter. Jaume hadn't moved and was still straddling the strap that had gone between his legs, which now made two separate circles connecting to the life preserver, and as I looked at Jaume's muscular thighs I imagined him as the famed Colossos of Rhodes straddling the strait. What a sight it must have been to sail between those massive thighs and gaze upwards!

I reached down and fondled Jaume's cock through the fabric of his green swimsuit, staring defiantly at the men around us. Like me, Jaume was half-hard already and I could feel his dick respond to my fingers. The men said nothing, content, it seemed, to be voyeurs and nothing more. Even the blond in the orange bathing suit was silent, although he watched my hand as it moved, looking up every now and then to meet my stare and then letting his gaze drop once more. Finally, he moved closer to us and dropped to his knees before Jaume. I pulled the green nylon down over Jaume's hips and his cock sprang free of the confining fabric. The blond reached out to hold it, and I looked up at the crowd around us, expecting them to respond in some way, but they were all as still as statues. It would've been much more normal for them to try and be involved, or to comment in some way, to have some sort of indication that they were, if not exactly participating, at least to show that they were present and aware. Even were they to pointedly ignore us, carrying on their conversation as if we were not fornicating in their midst would be a more direct acknowledgment.

I put them out of mind and looked down at Jaume's ass clenching and unclenching as he thrust his cock into the blond's mouth. My cock grew longer at the sight of my lover's cock being worshipped by this stranger's mouth, and it poked out from the side of my swimsuit. I still had my life preserver on, so I couldn't actually pull them down the way I'd done with Jaume, since the strap that ran between my legs prevented this. But I pulled my cock and balls free through one of the leg holes and started pulling at my dick; I didn't want to bother with the hassle of untangling the preserver, and the tight fabric of the swimsuit's leg hole against the base of my cock was a pleasurable pressure.

The blond still wore his orange swimtrunks as he sucked off my boyfriend, I noticed, and as if my glancing at his cock awakened some sixth sense in him he seemed to realize that my cock was also loose and seeking for attention, and without either looking up or breaking his rhythmic motions along Jaume's cock, he reached out and grabbed hold of my cock with unerring precision, as if he'd all this time been completely aware of where it was in relation to him. This was a skill I'd often admired in men who had it, like the ability to locate another man's nipples through his shirt without groping around to figure out where they were.

I looked up again at the men around us as the blond jerked on my dick, but it was as if time had been stopped as far as they were concerned, for all the life they showed. I glanced at their crotches, to see if at least we were providing them with a good spectacle, but it was hard to tell if they were aroused or not. As if he could tell my attention had wandered away, the blond's tugging at my dick changed, and suddenly he pulled me forward by my cock until I had to shift my stance;

I stumbled forward and suddenly I was sliding into the wet of his mouth. I watched his lips work their way up and down my shaft, and looking past his face I could see the outline of his own dick, obviously hard, within his orange swimsuit. But he made no move to take it out or even touch himself through the fabric. I was glad, judging from his arousal, that he was obviously enjoying some aspect of this scene. And then I closed my eyes and stopped worrying and let myself enjoy the slippery magic of his tongue on my cock. With my eyes still closed I reached out and found Jaume's pierced tit, as if I'd suddenly acquired that skill that had always amazed me, although I think it was simply because the piercing made for a much larger area for my fingers to find. I tugged at the silver loop gently and smiled and opened my eyes and found my lover was smiling at me back. I grabbed him by the neck and pulled him toward me for a kiss.

Below us, the blond had grabbed both of our dicks and was jerking us off as he caught his breath. Or perhaps he was simply considering, weighing our cocks in his fists as he contemplated his next move. He tugged our cocks until we were standing close to one another, then put both of us in his mouth at once. It's a strange feeling, because it's not as wonderful as having a pair of lips clamped tightly around the shaft of your cock, but at the same time sharing something so intimate with my lover made the experience even more intense. Jaume's and my own tongues locked as the blond ran his back and forth over the sensitive crowns, pulled free from their foreskin by the state of our arousal. I could feel my breath quicken in those moments leading up to orgasm, and I grabbed my own dick with one hand and began to jerk myself off. Jaume followed suit, and I looked down at the blond, to see how he was responding, imagining he might be touching himself, but he seemed to be just watching us jerk off and enjoying the sight from his crotch-eye view. But then he leaned forward and began to suck on my balls, and after a few more moments I was sending short white arcs of cum onto the wooden deck. I made a sort of grunt into Jaume's throat with each spasm that went through my cock, and even with my eyes closed in ecstasy I could tell that Jaume had quickened the pace of his hand's motion. Soon his tongue was pressing deeply into my mouth as he, too, came.

The blond was still kneeling before us, smiling widely. And suddenly, now that the sex was over, the other passengers suddenly came to life. I didn't quite understand the noise at first, lost in the afterglow of orgasm, but I soon made out words, and realized they were talking to each other again, and going about things as usual, although still keeping an eye turned toward us every now and then. Maybe it was because Jaume and my cock were still bare for all to see, mine already shrinking now that I'd cum but Jaume's still a rigid pole; he always took a while for it to go down. "Well that was certainly worth a first class trip to the shore," I announced. The blond smiled again, and climbed to his feet. I wondered for a moment if he were planning to kiss us, and half hoped he would, it would make the encounter feel suddenly more... personable. But the moment passed and he turned toward the others.

Jaume bent forward and pulled his swimsuit up to cover it and then stepped into the loops of the life preserver. I helped him into it, as the blond said goodbye to his friends. I watched him kiss them farewell, some on either cheek and some directly on the lips, and wondered what each man must feel, knowing where his mouth has been just moments before. Were they disgusted? Jealous? Indifferent, as they'd been while watching us? I wasn't sure. And it didn't really matter.

Jaume and I descended first to resume our places at the oars. I wondered, for a moment, what would happen if we simply took off before the blond descended. It was not as if there were anything truly binding us to wait for him, other than our word. What could he do, complain to the police that he had given us each blow jobs and we wouldn't take him to shore in return? It wasn't as if he'd dive in after us, since he was afraid of the jellyfish. And with reason, I noticed, watching a ghostly white shadow bloom in the water just beside our kayak.

We waited for him, an honorable exchange as we'd agreed, and once he'd settled himself on the little ridge between Jaume and my seats we began paddling and pulled away from the boat. His friends called out after him, and there were other shouts and noises and the sounds of frivolity from men we couldn't see from our lower vantage. Suddenly the boat seemed like a lively and fun place, quite the opposite of how it'd been when we'd been aboard. Had we been the inhibiting force? I wondered. Or maybe it was our passenger? Again, I thought, it didn't really matter. My lover and I had enjoyed our private encounter there amidst the crowd, and I at least had no regrets.

Our strokes had pulled us nearly to the shore. "Thanks," our passenger said as he leaped off the kayak into the shallow water and waded the last few feet onto the sandy beach. He turned around and waved at us, and back at the ship, and then walked off up the sand. I wondered briefly what plans he had here, if maybe we'd see him again later at the dance. Or any of those men from the boat...

One of the Kayak crewmen came jogging over and yelled at us for coming this close to the beach and told us we had to head out to deeper waters or bring the kayak back to the launch. We pushed off, Jaume and I, paddling back out among the higher waves and the ghostly jellyfish. The sky was crystal blue, the sea was warm, my boyfriend was with me and we'd just had a threesome with a sexy blond, on the beach behind us was a party celebrating being gay: it was one of those perfect moments.

We weren't paddling in any direction, just sort of enjoying

being out on the surf. After a while, Jaume looked over his shoulder at me and asked, "Think we should go back to the boat and see if anyone else needs a lift?"

   I smiled at Jaume, and without a word I stuck my oar into the water like a rudder again, turning our course back toward the ship at my lover's request.

The River of Time

I placed Eric's ashes on the seat beside me. I wasn't expecting to feel such relief to let go of them, which made me realize it was the right thing to do. I'd been carrying them around for so long, it seemed, walking through this last request he'd made to me: to scatter his ashes from the Christopher Street Pier into the Hudson River. I knew I was having trouble letting go of him. I'd kept putting off the day of scattering his remains with excuses: the weather wasn't right for how I thought his last moment (as if he hadn't already had it) should be or my work schedule meant I couldn't do it at the "right" time of day for such an occasion, whatever it took to convince myself of the need to delay.

Now that my hands were free, I rubbed my shoulders, which ached from the weight of carrying him around. The urn with his ashes was nothing, really, compared to what his physical presence had been. I was amazed that an entire human body could become so insubstantial.

"We're mostly water," Eric had said, the first time he'd gotten really sick, when he was telling me what he wanted me to do. "They'll just be taking all the water out. I'll be like that freeze-dried food they give astronauts. Just add water and it pops back to life."

I didn't say anything. There was nothing I could say that would change anything, make a difference. He'd put his hand on mine and continued. "That's why I want you to dump me in the river. I know I won't pop back to life, not like that astronaut food. But it'll be like mixing me up into a sort of clay and giving me a new start. Who knows where I'll wind up? I want to go all over the world, at last get to visit all those places I never could afford to go to! And I will; I'll be like a drop of ink falling into a cup and, over time, it colors the entire glass. You'll never be able to see water, drink water, even *be* water, since that's what you mostly are—anywhere there's water, I'll be there, too."

I'd started to cry, and he stopped talking to stare at me. I'd laughed at myself then, I'm not sure why, the look on his face or my lack of control or both, and he'd reached out with one arm to wipe a tear from my cheek. "Anywhere," he said, holding the salty tear on his finger.

He'd gotten better, only got that sick once more. But he never let it stop him; he was always living grandly, by the seat of his pants, getting into scrapes, having adventures—even those two times he was confined to a hospital bed. That first time, when he spent a week in St. Vincent's, he'd seduced one of the male nurses, who'd broken all sorts of rules and regulations to finger-fuck him and jerk him off. There were boxes of safety rubber gloves everywhere, and medicinal lubricants. He'd claimed it was some of the best sex he'd ever had, as he gleefully told us the details one night at the restaurant.

Eric had been one of the protease success stories. He'd seemed invulnerable—except for those two hospitalizations—as he confronted elemental forces of nature: he went white water rafting, climbed mountains, went deep water scuba diving, anything and everything that would give him that terrifying, exuberating thrill. We'd all gotten used to the idea that this disease would kill him in the end, despite the drugs, as the promise of a cure kept slipping further and further back. But it had been such a shock for him to die as he had, a freak accident in his own home where he'd tripped getting out of the bathtub and cracked his skull, something having nothing to do with his HIV.

We felt cheated, I guess. At least I did. We'd always thought there'd be time to say goodbye, a long slow descent. His friend Liza had asked him once, when a group of us were getting stoned at her apartment late at night, how he felt about suicide, if he thought there might be a point when he'd want it for himself.

He hadn't answered right away. Sitting up, he looked around, took another hit. "I'm too much of an overachiever ever to give up," he'd said. "By the time I got so bad that I'd want suicide, I wouldn't be able to do it myself." He'd smiled then. "I'd feel like such a failure if I had to have someone help me, I'd never be able to live with myself."

I wasn't sure why he'd picked me. We were friends, but in a casual sort of way. We were never lovers, though sometimes we flirted so madly that our acquaintances were sure we were getting it on with one another. I met him one night when I was working as a waiter at Stingy LuLu's and he'd come in and just struck up a conversation with me every time I walked past, not hitting on me, just talk. He became a "regular" and somehow that evolved into a friendship, where we'd see each other outside the restaurant. And whenever I quit and started working elsewhere, he'd become a regular over there. He had an amazing appetite and would try anything you put in front of him, which made sense given how adventuresome he was in other parts of his life.

"Why the Hudson?" I'd asked him one time.

"Exactly!" he'd replied, and I knew there was a doozy of an explanation coming. Eric was always enthusiastic when he was telling of his exploits, and this, to him, was just one more adventure. "Who'd even notice me in there, what with all the pollution and stuff? It's someplace I've always been too afraid to go swimming, but when I'm dead I won't be so afraid. It beats getting flushed down the toilet like an alligator.

"Besides, I think it's the perfect place for my ashes to be dumped, because whenever *I* got dumped, that's where I always went: down to the piers, to drown my sorrows and the memory of my now-ex-boyfriend in the sticky, blissful forgetting of anonymous sex."

So he and I were on our last excursion together, taking the subway downtown to go dump him in the river like he wanted.

Walking through the street with his ashes had felt uncomfortable at first, like when I had just realized I was gay and was afraid that everyone else could tell, too, like it was written on my face the way some of the kids at school would write signs saying KICK ME and tape them on my back when I wasn't looking. I walked around with this awkward burden that was all that remained of my friend as if it were some secret shame; everyone who passed me stared at it, recognized what it was. When they looked at me, it was as if they thought I had murdered him, as if I were holding his dripping severed head in my hands. They wouldn't meet my eyes.

But as I kept walking, there began to be something liberating about carrying Eric's ashes, as if I were showing him one last good time. It was the in-your-face, I'm out and proud defiance of being queer, and it felt right. People still looked at me, but now they were the ones to look away, and I knew they were thinking about their own mortality, or of family or friends. I know that seeing me carrying Eric's ashes had changed them—or at least some of them. So many New Yorkers have blinders on when they walk the streets: don't look, don't get involved. I wanted to go up to them and shake the urn of ashes in their face—but I felt that wouldn't be right to do to Eric. I was acutely aware of what I held, careful to not jostle the contents of the container I carried, even though I felt pretty sure Eric didn't mind, or didn't care, or wouldn't even notice.

Trying to maneuver through the subway turnstile had been tricky, dropping the token in the slot with one hand while trying hard to not bang Eric against the metal and rattle him. As we passed through, I couldn't help silently wondering if I should use two tokens. I smiled at my joke, despite the macabre humor of it, then felt guilty for smiling. I tried to reason that this was exactly the kind of humor Eric had liked and used himself, but I felt like I was trying to convince myself. I wasn't Eric, and just to have had the thought made me blush.

I'd kept the urn on my lap when I first sat down, since I felt guilty taking up two seats on the subway. But this was Eric's last chance, really, to take up space in this world. Now Eric sat beside me as if he and I were going downtown to shop or cruise, any ordinary Sunday afternoon.

"When my husband passed away, I had him cremated," the woman across the aisle from me said. I felt like everyone on the car turned to stare at me, and what I held. Why didn't they look at *her*, I wondered, this middle-aged white woman who sat opposite me; she was the one speaking, making noise, attracting attention. I looked away from her, hoping she'd stop talking to me, I didn't want to hear, didn't want everyone else to hear. But she continued. "They put him in a little box, nothing so fancy as that. I didn't believe he was really all in there, it was such a tiny thing. So I looked inside, and there was a plastic baggie in there! With all the ashes inside the little ziploc baggie."

I'd wanted to peek inside, too, to make sure the ashes were really in there. But I'd resisted. It seemed only bad things could come of such mistrust. I thought of all the stories of men who'd looked too soon, and lived to regret it: Lot, looking back and turning his wife into a pillar of salt; Orpheus, fearing she wasn't following him from the underworld, and then losing her forever.

I grabbed the urn and stood up, even though the train hadn't stopped, anticipating my exit. I felt guilty at turning my back on her—the opposite of those stories from the bible and myth—but I just couldn't deal with this right now. The subway pulled to a stop. The doors opened and I leapt through them, brushing past the people waiting to board.

On the street, I slowed down, took a deep breath. This was Eric's last trip down this historic gay street, I realized, and I wanted him to get a good last look. I held the urn up in front of me as I walked past St. John's Church in the Village. Again passersby looked at us. Some looked away when they realized what I held, others smiled. I didn't really care what either set thought, I did this for Eric.

We crossed Bleeker Street. There, across the street, was the Village Army Navy, the Potbelly Stove Cafe, Don't Panic; we passed McNulty's Rare Teas Choice Coffees Since 1895, The Leatherman, the Hangar bar, the Lucille Lortel Theater; at the corner of Hudson, the infamous Christopher Street Bookshop. I wondered briefly if I should walk inside, realized how foolish I'd feel going in there holding a funerary urn filled with ashes. In so many ways, this entire nostalgia inventory felt forced, as if I were making a ritual of this all because I, too, was losing these places, as if I couldn't visit or enjoy them after this last journey because Eric was no longer alive to share them with me. As if he'd ever been such a large part of my life; dead, he took up more of my time and thoughts than he had when he was alive!

I continued on toward the water, past the homeboys sitting on the steps at the PATH entrance, past the other erotic video stores and bars, across the highway and onto the piers at last.

Lots of men were just hanging around, their shirts off, some smoking weed, listening to boomboxes. Men and women on rollerblades skated past people out jogging or walking their dogs. I walked down to the end, climbed through a hole in the chain link that stretched up over the protective concrete partition. There were a handful of us out on this "forbidden" zone of the pier, no barrier between us and the crumbling edge that led to the water.

This was it. The moment of truth.

I looked down at the urn's closed lid. Eric had chosen and paid for it when he first got sick, so even though he hadn't expected to trip and die in his bathtub, he'd been prepared. An only son, his parents having predeceased him, and without a longterm lover, he had wanted to make sure his remains were taken care of.

"I want an urn fit for a queen!" he'd declared, when the salesman showed him the possibilities. He chose a Grecian-styled urn with a simple geometric design around it.

"I'd wanted one of the naughty ones," he'd confided to me, later, when he showed me the pictures. "You know, like they have at the Met, in that wing where you walk about in between sucking men off in the lavatory." He'd smiled lasciviously and sighed, "Ah, culture!"

I took the lid off. The inside was filled with a pale gray powder, finer than sand. It wasn't what I'd been expecting, which was flakier, more like charred paper, the way a book or log that had been burned looked, still having the semblance of form but crumbling at a touch.

It wasn't in a baggie, just loose ash inside the jar. I reached in, stood like that for a moment, my hand deep inside the remains of my friend. Then I pulled back, scooping up some ash, and held my hand out before me.

The fine powder drifted from my fingers, down to the choppy waves which looked, because of the light, like a hammered sheet of metal, solid, even though it was in constant motion, flux. I felt like I was adding powdered sugar to the top of an obsidian cake. Or more like adding salt to a soup, since the ash was sucked up greedily by the water, leaving no trace of itself on that restless surface. Handful after handful, I let go of the gray powder, as if I were desperate for seasoning, for flavor, for taste.

The ashes were not all thin powder. Sometimes there were larger chunks, like hard white pebbles, the kind that always get in your shoes when you walk on the beach or along a riverbank. I tried not to look at them. My hand moved mechanically between the urn's mouth and the sea, my eyes fixed on the point where the ash disappeared into the water.

A sudden gust of wind blew one handful back at me. I was blinded by the white flash of ash in my eyes, sputtered against the taste of it in my mouth. Frantically, I rubbed at my face with my hand, before I realized that it, too, was covered in ash, even the back. I put the urn down and rubbed at my eyes with the back of my left hand, wondering if I could catch HIV because I'd gotten ash in my eyes—a mucous membrane—the way semen in your eye could infect you. I hated myself for having the thought, knowing there was nothing of the virus that could survive the cremation, but I couldn't stop thinking it.

I remembered Eric, that afternoon when he first told me what he wanted me to do, brushing away one of my tears with his fingertip.

Now, for some reason, I couldn't cry. Even despite the ash in my eyes.

The noise and life of everyone around me came crashing back in on me, reminding me I wasn't alone, that life still went on—for me, for them, for us.

I stood and again picked up the urn. I reached inside; it was more than half empty now. Slowly, handful by handful, I released Eric's ashes into the Hudson River. I was never tempted to just overturn the urn I held and plop them all in at once.

As I scattered his remains, I remembered the good times we'd had together—a cliché, perhaps, but something I felt obliged to do: to think about him, us, what I'd miss about him. It wasn't difficult to remember happy moments; we didn't have many bad times together. I didn't see all that much of him, and he was always so good-natured and happy-go-lucky, it was hard to find him in a mood where he rubbed you the wrong way.

When the urn was empty, I stood there for a long while, just lost in thought, letting it sink in that he was finally gone.

I looked down at the empty urn, wondering what I should do with it. This was something that never got mentioned when people talked about scattering someone's ashes. It didn't feel right to just throw it out, especially since Eric had picked it out specifically. I turned my back on the water and climbed over the barricade and started walking down the pier again toward the city. I took the urn with me; I didn't know what else to do with it.

The entire trip back I was afraid to touch anything, afraid of leaving behind some trace of Eric like fingerprints lingering after a crime. I held the emptied urn in my right hand; since it was already filled with a trace of ash coating its insides, it wouldn't matter if some got on the outside, too.

If the pier hadn't been so high up from the water, I'd have knelt down and dipped my hand in the water, drawn up water into the urn to empty its clay belly, so all of Eric's ash was dumped in the Hudson as he'd wanted. I felt strange that I still carried some of him with me, as if I'd somehow failed in completing his final request. All I wanted now that I'd done the deed was to get home.

I got off the subway at Times Square, climbed upstairs, and started walking west. The urn seemed heavier than when it had been filled with ashes. I wanted to switch hands; my right arm was aching from carrying it for so long, supporting its weight without the help of my other arm. I rested the urn against my hip, or stopped and set it down on top of a trash can, but I didn't touch it with my other hand, as if it were now tainted. Ridiculous thoughts, I knew, but it was as if an immutable superstition had sprung up and I had to obey it.

   I didn't know what I planned to do when I got home, how that would change things somehow, but I felt that once I got there everything would be OK. I'd be safe.

   I lived in a fifth floor walkup in Hell's Kitchen, between Ninth and Tenth Avenues. It was a one-bedroom apartment, an illegal sublet from my downstairs neighbor, George, who was a painter. Evidently, he was a good enough painter that he could afford to own two apartments, or more likely he'd been something before he became a painter—an investment banker or lawyer—and earned enough to let him follow such rarely-lucrative pursuits as fine art painting. Whichever it was, I didn't care; the rent I paid was dirt cheap because I let him use my apartment as storage for his works. He hung his paintings—enormous abstracts with words hidden in them—on every wall, making my apartment a sort of mini-gallery dedicated to him. Except no one but me and my friends ever saw it; he never asked to bring anyone up and show them the paintings. And in the two years I'd been living there, he'd only once sold one of the paintings in my apartment. It was strange for the first month, to be staring at a new word—DISINTERESTED—above the television, day in and day out; I kept looking for the old word hidden somewhere in the painting, but of course never found it.

   I fished my keys out of my pocket with my left hand, and opened the three sets of locks on the door. When the door had closed behind me, I put the chain on and went directly into the bathroom. I placed the urn in the tub, as I would with anything dirty I brought into the apartment and meant to clean before I set it down on my own furniture or stuff. This wasn't something dirty. This was my friend, the last bit of him I still had, except for my memories, already beginning to fade as if my trying to recall them, my going over them again and again as I emptied the urn, had worn them out.

I sat down on the tub's cold rim and thought of how Eric had tripped and fallen, wondering what his last thoughts might have been, if he regretted dying in such an awkward, tawdry fashion instead of doing something daring and exciting. Shallow thoughts for someone to have while dying, perhaps, but they seemed appropriate somehow.

I leaned forward and turned the faucet on, with my left hand so as not to smudge ash everywhere. I stared at the burst of water, letting the rust run out. When it was rushing clear and cold, I ran my hand under it, washing the gray-white dust from my skin. I remembered letting my friend Phillip, an avant-garde sculptor I met when I was living in the East Village, take a plaster of paris cast of my hand for a project he was doing. I imagined Eric's ashes becoming sticky substance like that, mixing to form a clay—like he had said would happen, that day he first asked me to be responsible for scattering his ashes into the river. He said he'd become clay when he hit the water, so he could be shaped into a mannikin again and have life breathed back into him.

I picked up the clay urn he had chosen as his penultimate resting place. What would I do with it now? I set its lid beside me on the rim of the tub and held its wide mouth under the faucet. The urn was becoming Eric in my mind, my refusal to let go of it, as if it still held his ash inside. But why was it so important for me to keep it? His ash had never been him, even if it was the stuff that had once made up his body; the Eric I missed was something more, something ineffable and indescribable, something irrevocably lost.

As I was about to pour out the urn's contents, I was struck

by the face reflected in the water of its mouth: it wasn't my own.

I looked more closely, and sure enough, Eric looked back at me, just as if I were Eric, staring down into the water. Eric was young again, maybe ten years old. Something moved in the water, above the reflection: the shadow of a bird flying overhead. We were on a riverbank, looking into the water; I could see trees reflected behind us. I could feel the sun shining warmly on our back as we leaned over the river. Dark shapes flitted beneath the surface, and our eyes shifted from the reflection on the surface to what lay beneath. Fat little tadpoles bumped among the rocks on the riverbottom.

Where were we? How could this be real? Was this Eric's past? How was I here?

I reached out, in wonder, to touch his face, reflected in the water's mirror.

But as my fingers touched the reflection, the spell was broken, and I was in my bathroom in my apartment in Hell's Kitchen in New York City, sitting on the edge of my bathtub, staring down at the urn which had held Eric's ashes, now filled with a mix of water and the last traces of his gray remains that I'd been about to pour away.

I remembered Eric saying, "It beats getting flushed down the toilet like an alligator," and suddenly I couldn't just pour out this last bit of him down the drain.

What just happened? I wondered. What did this mean?

I wanted him back so badly I was hallucinating.

I wanted to hold onto him, this one little piece of him that was all I had left of him. Suddenly I wanted to hold him, like I'd never actually held him in life, though we'd always joked that one day we would have sex with one another, some night when we were drunk or stoned or just plain horny and happy and falling into one another's arms.

I turned off the faucet, which had been running all this time, however long I'd been lost in my daydreams of Eric. I lifted the urn from the tub and set it on the foot towel, to dry off its bottom and sides. I carried it out into the living room and set it on the small endtable, so it was sort of under both the window and the orange painting above the couch with the word INVINCIBLE hidden within its swirls of color.

I left the urn and went into my bedroom. I flopped down on the bed, wondering what was going on. Why was I feeling such strong emotion for Eric? Why now, when it was too late? Was it only because it was too late? Was this some expression of all my stored up grief, about everything, finding an outlet at last?

I felt worn out, drained, even though I'd only been up for a few hours. I sat up, looked at the clock, then reached over and set it to wake me up in an hour. I lay down again, thinking over the events of the past few hours, and especially the past few moments. I tried to match the place in my vision with some story Eric might've told me one night, but I couldn't figure out where it was, what adventure took place in that setting.

I must've fallen asleep, because I woke again when the alarm went off. It was time to head back downtown. I had to work dinner tonight at Pad Thai, the chic Chelsea restaurant on Eight Avenue. "Cute Boys and Asian Noodles" Liza always referred to it, teasingly, but with affection.

If I had dreamed, during my brief nap, I didn't remember anything from them. I felt a little disappointed, after the vivid images I'd seen while still awake.

I glanced at the urn on my way out of the apartment, but I didn't look inside it. I was too afraid of what I might see. And I was half-afraid that I wouldn't see anything.

All night long, I kept expecting Eric to come into the restaurant—alone, or with some friends, with a trick, it didn't matter. I just had a feeling that he'd stop by.

He didn't, of course. He was dead. I had held his ashes in my hands. But my mind refused to admit it; I hadn't seen the body before it was cremated, didn't really have proof that he was forever gone, and not simply out of town on one of his wilderness excursions.

I was in a fog at work, messing up people's orders, making the wrong change. I stumbled home, wearily unlocked the three locks, looked at the urn from across the room, then went into my bedroom and shut the door.

The alarm went off. I woke with a piss boner, and as ever I wondered if there had been some sort of mental erotic stimulation in my unremembered dreams, or if it was merely a quirk of bodily function. As I lay in bed, feeling my hardon begin to subside a little and the pressure on my bladder increase, I felt like everything was back to normal again. That somehow, despite having finally let go of Eric's ashes, despite that strange episode last night where it had seemed like I saw his ghost—or his past—life would now go on as ordinarily as ever.

And, just like ever, if I didn't get out of bed and showered I was going to be late for class. I was studying intermediate German at Baruch College, and even though I was taking the course through their Adult Education division, because of my schedule they let me take the regular undergrad class which met first thing in the morning. Last year I had fallen in love with this boy from Berlin who was visiting New York for a week. He'd given me his address, in case I ever came to Germany, and in the weeks after he left I looked around desperately for a course in basic German, thinking I would move there to be with him, I could work in a hotel, they always had a need for English-speakers, I would figure it out later, all that mattered was that I be with him. He never answered my letters, but by then I was already beginning to learn the language, and decided to stick with it to spite him. Maybe one day I would go to Germany anyway, and work in a hotel, and fall in love with someone.

At least, it had seemed like a good idea at the time, but now, if I didn't wake up, I'd be late to class. I took a piss, and turned the water in the shower on. While waiting for the water to heat up, I went into the kitchen and put on a pot of coffee. On my way back through the living room, I looked inside the water-filled urn.

There was motion on the bottom, and I thought at first that it must be a swirl of ash floating inside the urn. But it was black, not gray. I thought this might be another vision, like the one last night. But I was still aware of myself—standing in my boxers, my early-morning breath—staring down at the urn.

The black shape moved, and I realized it was a fish. It swam around in circles. No shit, Sherlock, I told myself, realizing there was nothing else for it do given the shape of where it was swimming. I'm always something of a bitch before I've had my coffee. Especially when I'm hallucinating against my will and without the aid of drugs.

I reached out and touched the surface of the water, expecting the vision to vanish as the one last night had done. It didn't. The little fish swam up toward my finger, and I pulled back before I got bitten. Not that such a tiny fish—smaller than my pinkie—could've done much damage.

It swam to the surface, as if to beg for food, and I realized it was a tadpole, not a fish, like the ones Eric had been staring at last night in the vision.

What did it mean? I didn't have the inkling of an idea, certainly not when it was still so early in the morning.

I wondered what human foods tadpoles could eat, and remembered throwing stale bread and crackers to fish at ponds when I was younger. But looking down at it, swimming in circles, I also remembered that tadpoles didn't eat, they just digested their own tails, transforming themselves into frogs that way.

In German class, we'd been reading some of the Grimm fairy tales in German, including "The Frog Prince," where a frog gets transformed into a prince. In the version I knew from my childhood, this magical transformation was because of a kiss, but in the story we read the frog was thrown against the princess' wall, after eating from her plate and drinking from her cup, which turned him back into human form.

Had Eric been transformed into this tadpole, who'd grow up to be a frog—and perhaps, if kissed by a boy who loved him, into a human prince?

What had Eric been doing by that riverside, in the vision I'd had of him? Had he been looking to catch a frog to kiss?

It was too early for me to be thinking, let alone trying to puzzle out such strange mysterious things as unasked for visions and the sudden appearance of this tadpole from one of them.

I went into the bathroom and took a shower, constantly aware of the fact that Eric, when last he was in his bathroom, had tripped getting out of the tub and cracked his skull. My heart raced when shampoo dripped in my eyes and I was suddenly blinded, feeling off-balance as I turned to hold my face up to the falling water.

I didn't slip, didn't die. I dried off, got dressed, drank my coffee. I looked at the urn on the table under the painting, and tried not to puzzle over what was going on; perhaps if I just let things happen, it would all become clear soon enough. That's how I'd first learned to find the words hidden in George's paintings, to just look at them until eventually, suddenly, they made sense.

I left for class, thinking about Uwe from Berlin, who I hadn't thought about in a long time.

The tadpole was still there, swimming in circles inside the urn that had held Eric's ashes, after class. Fraulein Staudacher had been impressed by my sudden leap of fluency this morning, which had come upon me without warning. It was as if a switch had been thrown inside my brain; I didn't need to think about the individual words, just listened for—or spoke—the sentence as a whole, and somehow it all made sense. I think it was because I was in such a fog, I wound up inadvertently practicing that same philosophy I'd used to understand George's paintings. If I'd been more awake or aware, I'd have been too surprised by my ability to speak this strange tongue I didn't really know yet, and I'd have stumbled over my own tongue trying to figure out how and why I was talking so well this morning.

Maybe whatever magic had made this tadpole appear had given me the gift of tongues as well.

I had no idea why any of this was happening—the German, the tadpole, the visions—and I wondered: Why me?

It had something to do with Eric, that seemed to be obvious from the way everything had happened only after I'd scattered his ashes. Was there some curse haunting the urn, still—that bit of bad karma that had made him trip? Should I get rid of it before something untoward happened?

I looked down at the tadpole, trying to figure out what this all meant, if there was a purpose to my having these strange visions, which were leaking into the real world.

Or was it all a figment of my grief-stricken imagination? I reached toward the water, touched its surface, waiting for the tadpole to disappear as if it had never existed, a phantom trick of light on water. But beyond my fingers I could see it, swimming as if unconcerned by the presence of my hand in its bowl, the possibility of my grasping hold of it. I reached for the tadpole, but it managed to elude me, despite the tiny confines of the urn. I was determined to prove once and for all whether or not it was real by holding it in my hand. I reached and reached into the water, until my arm was deeper inside the urn than it could possibly be.

And suddenly I couldn't pull back. The water was pulling me onward, like a fierce undertow or a whirlpool dragging me into its depths, into the urn.

My hand closed about the tadpole at last.

Triumphant I lifted it above my head. I could feel it squirming inside my hand. Water dripped from my fingers, back into the river, rippling my reflection.

"What have you got, Eric?" a voice behind us asked.

It was Tom, Eric's camp counselor. He was older, maybe sixteen, seventeen. The other kids had gone with Jamie, the other counselor, to explore a cave that was nearby, but Eric had wanted to stay by the river. He couldn't be here alone, so Tom had stayed with him.

Our eyes were drawn to his crotch. He wore bright blue speedos, and the thick bulge of his cock was visible beneath the thin fabric. Tom rubbed his hand across the bulge with one hand.

"It's a tadpole," Eric said at last.

"Come here and show it to me," Tom said. He smiled, friendly, as we walked over to where he was sitting on a nearby rock. He took our closed fist in his big palm, and placed it in his lap. The bulge underneath his bathing suit pressed against the back of our hand.

Eric looked into Tom's eyes, over his shoulder, anywhere but into Tom's lap.

Tom slowly pried Eric's fingers open. Cool water dripped onto his lap, soaking into his bathing suit. The tadpole squirmed free and dropped into the space between Tom's legs.

Eric still wouldn't look into Tom's lap, and our heartbeat was thundering in our ears, suddenly audible.

Tom kept uncurling Eric's fingers, then turned Eric's hand over in his lap, until we were pressing against Tom's hard dick.

Tom was still smiling.

He held Eric's wrist, and slowly moved our arm back and forth, so we were rubbing against his dick.

"You want to see what I have?" Tom asked.

Eric didn't say anything. We couldn't speak. Our mouth was dry, as if we'd been bitten by a watersnake. Cottonmouth.

Tom hooked one hand under the brim of his bathing suit, and began to tug it down, still holding our hand pressed against his cock.

I leapt into the water to get away, diving into my reflection.

I was drenched.

What had just happened? I wondered, as I stood in my living room, one hand held just above the urn of water.

What had I just seen? Why was I having these visions of Eric's past—if it truly was his past, and not simply my subconscious in denial over his death, conjuring him again through these hallucinatory episodes.

How could any of this be real?

And how could I deny that it was real? My clothes were soaked through, I was dripping water onto the rug.

Where were these visions coming from, and why? Eric had never told me anything about camp, and I was afraid to continue having this vision, to follow it through to its painfully obvious and inevitable climax.

I walked into the bathroom, stripping off my wet clothes and leaving them in a pile on the tiled floor. To my surprise and chagrin, I had an erection from the strange rape-fantasy vision I'd just had. I felt myself blush with shame, even though there was no one who knew, no one there to witness my sexual excitement from something I found so morally unpleasant. But I felt like my body had betrayed me.

I turned the shower on, but sat on the rim of the tub, waiting for my hardon to go down. I didn't trust myself right now, I didn't know what my body did when I had these visions, was afraid of falling while I was in the tub as Eric had. And everything was all happening so quickly, so strangely, I felt bewildered. And resentful.

I stalked back into the other room, leaving the shower running. I was determined to throw the urn out, at the very least pour off the water. I never asked for these intrusions into my life.

But when I picked it up, stared down at the tadpole, still swimming in circles, innocent and unaware, I knew that I couldn't bring myself to pour it down the drain and kill it. Even while I seethed with rage at the things it was doing to my mind.

My skin felt sticky, the riverwater—or vision-water, whatever it was that had drenched me while I was in Eric's past—having dried in the warm Spring air.

I put the urn back on the endtable and went back into the bathroom. I stood under the showerhead for a long time, letting the hot water relax the tension from my back, trying not to think about anything except the fact that I was determinedly not thinking about anything. I couldn't help occasionally thinking about falling in the tub and cracking my skull, quick flashes of what it would be like, the dizzy tilting forward as the world, and my feet, slipped away.

I dried off, put on clean clothes. I sat on my bed, growing angry again by the thought that I was afraid to go into my own living room because of the urn and hating the feeling of being trapped, feeling like I had nowhere to go except in circles like that stupid tadpole.

I left early for work, locking the door behind me as if I could seal off this strange influence and abandon it here, in my home, the one place where I should feel safe from the rest of the world.

Michael kept trying to convince me to come out drinking with him after work, but I just didn't have the energy. I felt like I should go with him, do something with people, get my mind off Eric. But I just felt so drained, I wanted nothing but to finish work and go home and go to bed.

As a waiter, you get used to looking up whenever the door opens, to see how big a party it was, if nothing else, and make sure someone was there to seat them—preferably in your section if it was a party of four or more. But even though I'd mostly had tables of ones and twos tonight, I was glad when Tina sat this new group in Michael's section. As they were standing there, waiting for someone to help them, I couldn't help admiring the stunning black man with a shaved head, who noticed my attention and smiled. I didn't know what the arrangements were among the three of them: two women—one Asian and one white—and another black man, who could all just be friends, or possible partners, in whatever combinations. I couldn't even be sure he was gay, or at least bisexual, but I was pretty sure he was interested in me: there was that spark of interest there, that had me suddenly full of energy and excitement.

Michael noticed my revived spirits, and again asked me to come to Barracuda with him after work, but I put him off. He hadn't noticed why I was suddenly so alert, and I was content to let things remain that way. I knew they'd be teasing me for weeks if they saw me pick up one of the customers; that's what happened to any of us who got lucky while we were working.

I always find it tacky to try and pick up customers, or for people to try and pick up their waiter. It's an awkward situation, because you can't get out of it—from either side—until the meal's through. As a waiter, you try to be friendly, and even a little flirtatious for the sake of a tip. And because you're accessible to the public, it's best not to mix work with your personal life, because if things go sour, your ex can always track you down, cause a scene. Make things messy.

But this one was just too good to let slip away, and he

seemed to feel the same way about me. All while they ate he kept watching me, and I was happy to stare back at him, smiling, waiting. Which of us would make the first move?

I liked watching him move. He had a languid grace—even just while eating and talking—that kept catching my eye, the way he held himself as he sat, how his body unfolded itself along the bench. I wondered what he'd look like doing other things, imagined how his body would look without clothes. He wore comfortable, loose clothes, but I could tell he had a fine body underneath it, not overdeveloped like many of the men in Chelsea, but firm and taut. You could tell just from the way he held himself that he had muscles many of us only dreamed about, and he knew how to use them and keep them in shape.

I was glad for my apron hiding the hardon I was getting, fantasizing about him when I wasn't busy tending the needs of the customers at my few tables. I thought about going into the john and jerking off, but decided against it, enjoying the pleasurable tension of wanting release.

Thinking about going to the bathroom, however, made me recognize the growing pressure on my bladder.

"Cover for me," I told Tina, heading toward the back of the restaurant.

"Don't forget to wash up!" Michael called. I felt as if the entire restaurant turned to look at me.

I took a piss. I flushed. I washed my hands, wondering if I could get away with bringing a wet paper towel out and slapping it on Michael's arm, an innocent prank.

When I opened the door, the man was there, waiting as the next in line. I was surprised—and also pleased.

"Hey," he said.

"Hi."

We stood just looking at each other for a moment, and I snorted a little at the absurdity of breaking the ice, especially standing in the doorway to a lavatory.

"I know this sounds like a line," he said, "but you've got the most beautiful eyes."

I grinned, feeling good, one of those rare moments when the guy you want wants you back. I was so relieved he was willing to make the first moves. "Thanks," I said. "What if I hope that was a line?"

He smiled, too. "When do you get off work?"

I told him. He arranged to meet me at the Big Cup later tonight.

"I really do have to use the bathroom," he said, smiling again.

I laughed, and let him pass.

Marvin pinched my butt as we climbed the stairs to my apartment. "Stop that!" I cried, brushing the air behind me. He'd already let his hands drop to his side, all innocence.

I stopped on the landing and waited to ambush him, as he followed a few steps behind me. "You silly," I said. He was still one step below me, but our bodies felt so close together. I couldn't resist touching him, having wanted to do so all evening but feeling self conscious because we were in public. I leaned forward and our breaths mingled; I could smell the sweet spice of cinnamon and cappuccino on his breath.

And then our lips met, our first kiss, soft and exploratory, then growing bolder, stronger.

"Mmmmm," he replied, his tongue lost inside my mouth.

I pulled him closer, no longer caring who might see us—even my neighbors, who I'd have to see again in the morning, and for months to come. "You sexy silly," I said, running my hands from his shoulders down his back. His body felt as fine as I'd imagined it; he was a dancer, getting an MFA at Tisch, and his studies and practicing had paid off.

It felt so deliciously naughty to be so frisky with each other out here, with the chance of discovery by the neighbors, but there were things I wanted to do with him that I didn't want to be standing (in a stairwell no less) for, so we continued climbing to the top floor.

The door to my apartment opened when I leaned against it, preparing to put the first key into the hole.

Could George have, finally, decided to show off some of his paintings? Had he sold one, and needed to collect it immediately?

I pushed the door fully open, turned the light on, and looked cautiously inside.

"Shit!"

I'd been robbed. I could tell in an instant that they'd taken the easy stuff: TV, VCR, stereo. Items they could pawn easily on the street.

They'd left George's paintings.

I wondered if, perhaps, George had been the thief, unlikely though that seemed. The thought made me feel less violated, as if there might be some understandable (if not quite rational) explanation for all this.

But this had been a true break-in, out of the blue.

Almost literally. The kitchen window was wide open. They'd come down from the roof.

I'd thought I was safe up here, as opposed to the ground floor, say; there were bars over the bedroom window that led to the fire escape. Who knew they'd think my place was worth the effort of swinging down off the roof on a rope, so easily noticed by a neighbor or someone on the street, but no one ever looked up this high, not in this area. Tourists maybe, but they wouldn't be here.

"Shit," I said again.

They'd used my own garbage bags to carry the stuff out, so no one would know what it was. Even if you didn't know someone in your building, you wouldn't really look twice at someone taking out the trash. And they'd probably gone up on the roof, climbed across to one of the other buildings who all shared the same tar beach, and gone down that stairwell.

I paced from room to room, furious at this invasion, cataloguing in my mind what had been taken.

"They killed your fish," Marvin said.

I turned to look at him, surprised to find him kneeling on the floor of my living room, by the couch, this stranger I'd met tonight and brought home with me.

I'd forgotten about him.

I'd forgotten, too, about the urn.

Marvin was holding up the tadpole, dead and stiff, having drowned in air when the intruders knocked over the urn and spilled its contents onto the rug.

I wondered, for a moment, if the water had dripped through to George's apartment, if it had damaged any of his paintings. Implausible imaginings, the rational part of my brain knew: there wasn't enough water in the urn to soak all the way through the thick floors of this building.

But there'd been water enough to drench me completely, and still leave the urn filled to its wide brim, I remembered with a chill.

What was going on here? What was happening to me, because of this urn, because I'd kept this one piece of Eric? First the visions, then the tadpole, and now this theft and violation.

I picked up the urn. It was all because of this, I felt certain; this haunted, cursed receptacle.

It felt good to have something to blame. I carried it into the kitchen, wondering if I really dared throw it out the window, if that could truly dispel the bad karma that had been emanating from it ever since I'd emptied it of Eric's ashes.

I didn't understand why these things were happening. Was it because I kept the urn in the first place? Had I committed some celestial faux pas I wasn't aware of? Was I bringing this on myself by not letting go of Eric fully, leaving his spirit free to move on to its next adventure?

The burglary was so sudden and unexpected—like Eric's death had been. I wondered if this all had meaning; if I was supposed to learn something from all this.

It helped, somehow, to think that someone was putting me through this torture for a purpose. As if, having run this emotional gamut, I would be transformed. Like a frog, being kissed, turning into a prince.

"I'll understand if you want me to leave," Marvin said, following me into the kitchen. "It sort of kills the mood to come home and find this, doesn't it?"

I turned to look at him. Again, I'd forgotten he was there, even though I so wanted him to be here with me. I remembered how genuinely concerned he'd looked as he held up the dead tadpole, told me it was dead. It would never grow up and be transformed into a frog now, never have the chance to be kissed and feel like a prince, the way I'd felt in the stairwell with Marvin, as if we'd already found our happily ever after.

What was it about the blush of first intoxication that made it so sweet?

I didn't know if we'd see each other again, if we'd spend more than this one night together. If we'd even spend this night together.

I hoped we would.

Marvin seemed to be so much of what I'd been looking for. It was amazing to me that he could drop right into my life like this, even if for just a brief while. That connection, no matter how long, held power.

And I realized suddenly that not only bad things had happened because of the urn. What if my finding Marvin had also been caused by its strange mystical powers?

What if none of this had any connection to anything whatsoever? Just the random nature of the universe. A man falls in his bathtub. An apartment that's hardly worth the trouble gets burgled. A prince walks into my life.

Maybe this is what I was supposed to learn: that life doesn't make sense, you just have to make the best of it, and create the meaning from it that you want or need.

Marvin stood there, waiting for an answer. He was being so understanding, giving me space, but trying to be supportive. He looked so sexy, and also so warm and solid and real, an anchor in all this chaos.

A reminder that I was still alive.

"Please stay," I said, putting the urn down on the stove and walking over to him. I touched his shoulder, his cheek. "I don't want to be alone."

Thursday night, Marvin rang the street buzzer and I pressed the button to let him in. I grinned, eager to see him again; our first "date" even though we'd already had sex the night we met: exuberant uninhibited sex that made me feel I was reclaiming my apartment as my own space after the robbery, made me forget there was anything bad or ugly in the world. I imagined him climbing all those flights of steps, and wondered if he asked himself if the climb was worth it. It must've been, because he kept climbing. At last, I heard his footsteps growing nearer, and opened the door to greet him.

His face lit up when he saw me, which made me smile back as broadly. He stopped where he was, still a few steps shy of the landing, and let his tongue loll from his mouth as if he were a dog. He panted exaggeratedly, and said, "You, my friend, need an elevator."

I walked toward him, until we were in the position we'd been in when we'd first kissed, he a step below me. He put his arms around my waist, as I wrapped mine around his shoulders. His soft thick lips met mine, and I felt sexy and desired and magical.

He was carrying a bouquet of flowers, which he handed to

me: bright tiger lilies, just beginning to unfurl. I blushed, a happy warmth. I always feel shy when people give me flowers. I don't care if it's so traditionally heterosexual; I find it romantic.

He kissed me again, a longer kiss with tongue this time.

"I thought you could put them in that urn," Marvin said, following me inside, "since they killed your tadpole." I marveled that he was so comfortable with me already that he didn't feel awkward or self-conscious to refer casually to such a painful and awkward subject. I took a deep breath to calm the panic and anger that always wanted to overwhelm me at the thought of the robbery, that violation and disruption in my life. It felt so mature to be able to not get hysterical, and it was somewhat strange to realize that, of course I was mature, I was an adult; I still thought of myself as a teenager, just getting my feet wet in terms of accepting responsibility for my actions and such. I was still waiting tables, as if I were just out of college; what kind of a life was that?

I longed for the centeredness, the sense of having found yourself, which Marvin exuded. That was one of the things that made him so attractive; whether or not he actually felt that way, he acted as if he was always sure of himself, as if he had his feet planted squarely on the ground. While it all looked casual, you also got the feeling that nothing could knock him out of that stance easily. Some of it may have simply been his familiarity with his own body, its dancer's strength that left him feeling secure in what it could do.

I wasn't anywhere near that stable yet—physically or emotionally—but I felt like I was finally beginning to get there. Whether or not there was some celestial force testing me, the robbery was like a rite of passage—even if it had seemed like a baptism by fire at the time. I'd learned how to live with loss that night. Not just the loss of my stuff, but the loss of my friend, Eric. Even the loss of my magical tadpole, which I'd resented while it was impossibly manifesting itself in my life, unbidden and strange.

Now they were all gone, and I wasn't in a hurry to replace any of them, to go back to that state I'd been in before. As if earlier I'd been trying to regain the innocence—or ignorance—one lived in before death entered your life, like the time before losing your virginity, when even though you're constantly aware of sex, you don't know what it is actually like until you've had it, and then—whether the experience was good or bad—you're never the same again.

While I'd known people who were sick or dying before—relatives, acquaintances, whoever—Eric was the first of my peers that I'd actually lost. For a while, after he'd died, I'd been trying to live Eric's life in a way, to go on living it since he was no longer around to live it.

Somehow, like what had happened with George's paintings—or my German class—I'd learned to sit back and just accept everything until suddenly something went click in my head and it all made sense.

I did miss having my music, and I would get a new stereo. I didn't intend to deprive myself unduly to make some spiritual point that no one but me cared about or even knew was being made; I just hadn't gotten around to going shopping, too caught up in other aspects and details of my life.

"I've already found other uses for the urn," I said, leading Marvin into the kitchen.

I'd decided, in the end, to keep it. Not as some replacement or substitute for Eric, just as a sort of mnemonic, like keeping snapshots in a photo album.

Before work one evening, I'd bought soil from one of the gardening stores in Chelsea, then planted tomato seeds in the urn when I got home. The first tiny white roots had begun to emerge already, a rapidity of growth I attributed to Eric's influence.

Every time I watered them, I thought of Eric, that afternoon when he'd wiped a tear from my cheek and said, "Anywhere there's water, I'll be there, too. Anywhere."

And he was. In my memories of him. In the water.

And who knew, maybe one day it would feel right to fill the urn with water and find out what had happened to him that day at the river. Maybe that was why he'd asked me to be the one to scatter his ashes, knowing somehow—with the prescience of the dying?—that I'd thereby learn this story about his life that he couldn't tell me himself while he was alive. For all I knew, that moment in the vision might have a happy ending: his discovery that he was gay, that others had these same desires. Something I'd never considered while I was caught up in the visions themselves. I'd find out, one way or the other, if and when that day came.

In the meantime, the urn of future tomato plants sat on the kitchen windowsill. They would guard me against unwanted intruders, as best as they were able. That's all one could expect.

I set the bouquet of tiger lilies on the counter, then turned and gave my full attention to a welcome visitor to my home.

# Two Boys In Love
Carles & Javi

Can't Buy me Love

It was only as Carles placed the loaf of Silueta sliced wheat bread on the conveyor belt that he realized what he'd done. How could he have been so oblivious?

He quickly looked down into the green plastic carrier and pulled his few purchases from it, studiously avoiding the gaze of the man directly before him on line. It was perhaps the fourth time their paths had crossed here in the supermarket in the basement of the Callao El Corte Inglés, although never this directly. Not for lack of trying on the other man's part—he'd followed Carles up and down the aisles the first few times, constantly popping up just in front of him as if by chance, and all the while giving him the cruise of death.

Miguel Angel always teased him for shopping at El Corte Inglés, and even when Carles proved how shopping there selectively could be less expensive—the Silueta, for instance, was only 199 ptas at El Corte Inglés, compared to 325 ptas at the small panadería closest to his apartment in the Plaza Iglesia San Ildefonso—Miguel Angel still called him a wannabe pijo. It was certainly true that the people who shopped there were often of a certain social or at least economic standing, and included among their number a high proportion of homosexuals from nearby Chueca. Carles often found himself considering the other men who shopped there, judging them as much by their purchases as by their physical attractiveness. And just as often he found himself on the receiving end of someone else's scrutiny...

But Carles remained steadfast in his claim that he shopped there regularly because certain items were either less expensive or of higher quality than elsewhere, not to mention the convenience of being open at mid-day or late in the evening when Día or other supermarkets had already closed. Not that Carles was especially restricted in his available time to go shopping, since he worked out of his home and could pretty much decide his own hours, depending on his deadlines for delivering design projects to clients. So he actually shopped at all of the supermarkets: comparing prices, stocking up when items he liked were on sale, and so on.

Why had he decided to come to El Corte Inglés just then, instead of waiting until another supermarket opened at five? He could've waited until later and still shopped at El Corte Inglés... It was too late now, and Carles felt trapped. He only hoped the other man wouldn't try to talk to him.

"Muy rico el Toblerone!" the man said with enthusiasm, pointing to Carles' groceries. Despite his earlier resolution, Carles found himself looking up at the sound of the man's voice. His Spanish was obviously limited, and with a curious accent to it. French? Carles wondered. Maybe Swiss?

The man looked to be around forty, with a thick mass of wavy gray-brown hair that flopped into his face often and had to be pushed back. He had an exaggerated effeminate manner that irritated Carles, and had been one of the reasons Carles had never responded to the man's earlier advances. He was neither particularly attractive nor especially ugly, but there was something repellent about the man's deportment, Carles thought, almost as if he were a caricature of himself:

the foreign homosexual effete.

Carles found himself facing a dilemma. He did not want to encourage this man or get caught up in conversation with him, but neither did he wish to be uncivil, what with the cashier and other customers on line all within hearing. The Frenchman had him at a serious disadvantage—they were in public, and social niceties dictated that he respond. Although Carles was at a loss as to what he should say; the man's comment on chocolate was a non-sequitur.

"Te he visto antes aquí," the Frenchman continued, as if Carles had been holding up his half of the conversation.

"Yes," Carles replied, noncommittally, "we seem to shop at the same time."

The other man brightened noticeably at Carles' response.

"¿Tu eres de Madrid?" he inquired.

"No, from Valencia," Carles answered. He responded to the question and didn't offer anything more. Nor did he inquire further of his questioner, but the man responded as if Carles had done so.

"Yo soy de Lyon. Estoy aquí un mes. En el Hostal Hispano. ¿Lo conoces?"

The Hispano was one of the gay hostels in Chueca that advertised in all the free papers and guidebooks. Probably any homosexual who lived in Madrid and paid the least attention to the gay "scene" knew of it, or had at least seen it when walking down Hortaleza. What the man was asking, in an indirect way, was whether or not Carles was gay. But Carles did not want to play this game.

He was saved from having to answer by the cashier telling the Frenchman that his purchases came to 1765 ptas. The man took out a chargecard from his wallet, and also handed her his passport for ID. This is almost over, Carles thought with relief, as he watched the man place his groceries in bags. While they waited for his charge to clear the computer, the cashier looked between Carles and the other man with a knowing smile. Alarmed, Carles glanced up; the Frenchman was looking back at Carles with an expectant smile on his face. Carles looked away, afraid the man would continue to talk with him and was embarrassed that even the cashier recognized that he was trying to pick Carles up.

The Frenchman signed his name on the charge slip with a flourish and handed it back to the cashier. But he held onto the pen, and when she handed him back his card and his receipt, he wrote something on the back of the receipt and handed it to Carles. It was a mobile number. "Mi nombre es en el otro lado. Llámame." And he gathered up his bags with an air of triumph, as if it was a certainty that Carles would call him. Smiling over his shoulder half a dozen times, the Frenchman finally left.

Carles stuffed the receipt in his pocket, and glowered down at the cashier, who was smiling to herself and refusing to meet his eye as she rang up his purchases. "2347 ptas," she said at last, and Carles paid her in cash and hurriedly left behind those witnesses to his embarrassment. The cashier would probably repeat the story to the other cashiers later that evening, Carles thought, mortified. He'd need to make sure not to shop there at mid-day, to make sure he didn't shop there during her shift. And at least then he wouldn't cross paths again with that crazy Frenchman...

Suddenly, standing at the crosswalk waiting to cross Gran Via, Carles burst out laughing. How uncomfortable he'd been! But it was all over. And what did it matter if those cashiers enjoyed a joke at his expense? The whole situation had been rather comic, he could admit, now that he'd escaped it.

He was amused by the fact that the man had never even asked Carles' name. How would he know who Carles was if Carles did call him?

For that matter, Carles didn't know the name of who he'd be calling either, just his number. No, the man had said his name was on the receipt; it would've been printed out by the computer when the card cleared. Carles didn't even know why he'd kept the receipt, when he was certain he'd never call; politeness, maybe, to wait and throw it out when the man wasn't watching.

Out of curiosity, Carles put his bags down on one of the benches on the little sidestreet that ran behind Bash up to the Plaza de la Luna and took out the receipt, first lighting himself a cigarette as long as he had his hands free. The Frenchman's name was Christophe d'Aubigné. Carles was the sort of person who liked knowing people's names, and made an effort to remember them. In a way, knowing someone's name made him feel as if he had some sort of control over them; he knew how to refer to them when he thought about them, or had imaginary conversations with them.

Not that he planned to think much about this Christophe. Knowing his name would make it easier for Carles to forget about him.

Although he'd have to recount the story to some friends. Miguel Angel would say, of course, that Carles should've slept with the guy anyway. But then, Miguel Angel was less particular about who he slept with; anything male would do.

Carles remembered overhearing his younger sister and some friends talk about sex once. "Ugly men are better sex," one of them had said. "They try harder, because more is at stake for them."

"And they're usually more willing to go down on a girl," another had agreed. "Pretty boys just think about their own dicks, and if you're going to suck them or let them stick it in you. Ugly men also worry about whether you're feeling good."

His sister's friends might have a valid point there, Carles conceded. He certainly could recall many times when he'd found himself having sex with some gorgeous man at a sauna or back in the guy's apartment in the wee hours of the morning after leaving some club together, who simply lay there like a dead fish and expected to be worshipped. And other times when he'd been surprised at how good the sex was with men who he hadn't found all that attractive, who he thought held no "spark" of excitement for him.

But he still didn't plan to call Christophe. Although he found the man's persistence somewhat flattering. Especially when he'd given the man absolutely no encouragement. Carles didn't fancy himself that good-looking that men should behave in such a fashion. It was definitely good for the ego.

Carles liked that gay sex could be so easy to find sometimes. That if he'd wanted to, he could likely be in that man's hotel room right now, having his dick sucked. Or he could go to the Retiro and find someone looking for a bit of sex in the afternoon... But the truth was, Carles hated having to go looking for sex, although he'd done so often enough. It was one of the reasons he was glad to be in a relationship. Apart from simply being totally enamored of his boyfriend, Javi. He recalled how men were so often unwilling to hook up with someone at a disco until late in the morning; even if they were interested in you, it was as if they were leaving their options open in case something better came along. And by the time 4 or 5 AM rolled around, or later, and guys became willing to decide to go home with someone, Carles was usually worn out.

How ironic that now the opposite held true; he couldn't seem to get rid of his admirer. But that was often how life was, sometimes *las vacas flacas* and other times *las vacas gordas*.

Perhaps Carles needed to have been less polite and more forceful in his expression of disinterest—with some men it took something stronger than a polite no. Although, Carles had never yet said no, not outright, he had merely implied it. If it were up to him, he'd not have said anything at all to Christophe. Perhaps he should've been direct and said "I am not interested in having sex with you." But how embarrassing if Christophe had suddenly pretended that was not his intention at all! That he was merely trying to be friendly, to meet new people in this strange country he was visiting.

Whatever, Carles thought, and stepped on the glowing butt of his cigarette before gathering up his purchases and beginning the climb up the hill toward home. It was flattering to have an admirer, but he was happy to wait until next he saw his boyfriend to have sex. Despite what Miguel Angel had to say about his problem with jealousy and how to cure it.

A Movie Date

The brown bear and madroño tree, which together formed the emblem of Madrid, might both be nearly extinct in Madrid in real life, but the statue of them in Puerta del Sol served as one of the city's most popular meeting points. Carles, therefore, was unable to find a comfortable spot in which to stand or lean while waiting for Javi that was still in sight of the statue. Every available bit of wall was already occupied by other people waiting for someone to show up, as were the base of the statue itself, the nearby wooden planters that held live trees and greenery, the rear and sides of the magazine kiosks, and even the crossbars of the scaffolding on adjacent buildings. And then there were the crowds of people, moving through in one direction or the other or simply standing in groups and talking; Carles was buffeted from side to side, and finally let himself drift with the crowd, circling back again to stand before the statue when the tide of bodies had carried him too far adrift. It was easier than fighting to stay rooted in one spot against the irresistible onslaught of people.

He was early, which was usually the case when he'd

agreed to meet Javi, his eagerness to see his lover making him set off for their rendezvous far sooner than was necessary. Especially since Javi tended to show up ten to fifteen minutes late. Which was not really late, per se, but because Carles was usually waiting for an equal length of time before the appointed hour, by five or ten minutes past their meeting time he was usually fretting that Javi wouldn't show up. Even after so many months together, that uncontrollable fear still gripped him, and he had to fight it down as often as he fought to regain his position before the statue, waiting for his boyfriend to show up.

Carles stared at the queue outside Palazzo and contemplated joining it to order an ice cream cone himself, but decided against it. What if Javi arrived when he was inside and didn't find him? What if Javi thought he'd already gone and didn't wait?

Besides, he'd have popcorn at the theater, and they'd get a bite to eat later.

Where did all these people come from? Carles wondered. There were tiny ancient couples dressed in suits and lace dresses, long retired, who slowly walked arm in arm; tourists speaking in any of a dozen different languages; fad-following teenagers in their final days of classes; business men whose concession to evening had been to remove their ties; widows dressed in black; parents holding tightly to the hands of their young children, so they didn't wander off and get lost. There were people from all walks of life, and it sort of made sense that they would all meet here, at this cross-roads which was the literal center of Madrid, Km. 0, from which all paths were measured.

A pleasant Thursday evening in summer, only one day left in the work week and for many that was only a half day, it was only to be expected that so many people had gone out for a stroll, to see friends, to be seen.

The roar of a motorcycle drew the attention of Carles and

nearly everybody else in the Plaza. A path opened up before it, as it zoomed to a stop before the statue. But the crowd flowed into the open space almost immediately, erasing the cycle's path. Two men were riding it, wearing safety helmets that obscured their faces, one black, the other lime green. As their vehicle came to a rest, they both sat upright, and Carles saw that the driver was much taller than his companion, who dismounted. The second passenger took off his helmet and handed it to the other man, then turned and instinctively looked directly at Carles.

It was Javi.

The other man twisted in his seat without dismounting and locked Javi's black helmet in the box that rode at the back of the motorcycle. He didn't take off his own lime-green helmet, and didn't wait to be introduced to whoever Javi was meeting. He lifted one hand in a small farewell to Javi, then revved the engine again to alert the crowd to make way.

Carles wondered who Javi's friend was, as his boyfriend walked toward him.

Staring at the man's receding back as the motorcycle pulled away, Carles had a sudden gut feeling that, as impossible as it might appear, Javi's motorcyclist friend was David Beckham. Which would explain why he'd not removed his helmet, not wanting to be recognized in public.

It was impossible, Carles told himself. But the way the man had sat, after Javi had dismounted, his height, the way he carried himself, looked just like so many photos Carles had seen of him. Even without seeing the man's face, Carles was certain he was correct. It just felt like the only possibility.

This irrational fantasy was all Miguel Angel's fault, Carles knew. That morning, while they were putting together a grant proposal for a new AIDS-prevention campaign, Miguel Angel had gone on about this rumor he'd heard that David Beckham was having a gay affair. Which was just like his friend Miguel Angel, who had one of the most imaginative sexual fantasies of anyone Carles had ever met. It didn't matter that Beckham was not only married to ex-Spice Girl Victoria Adams but was rumored to have a girlfriend on the side, Miguel Angel saw every male as potentially gay.

And besides, ever since Beckham had moved to Madrid to play for the Real, Miguel Angel had been obsessed with maybe running into the man in person.

But what if the rumor were true?

And Carles' own boyfriend was somehow involved with him...

What a conflicting mix of emotions! Carles felt pride in Javi for being so handsome that even such a famous celebrity was interested in him, but he was also jealous, as always, of the idea of Javi with anyone else. And he felt a good deal of insecurity, since how could he compete with the famous athlete? What could he offer Javi that Beckham couldn't give him ten times over?

This is all ridiculous, Carles told himself, as Javi gave him a kiss on the lips. Javi was his boyfriend, no matter who else he might sometimes have sex with, and Javi was obviously willing to let the whole world know this, or at least as much of it as was crowded into Puerta del Sol just then, which felt like it amounted to a good portion of the population of Madrid. He was not ashamed of Carles, even if Javi did sometimes have sex with men who were more handsome, or richer, or more famous than his boyfriend was.

He and Javi turned together, after their kiss had ended, to walk toward Calle Montera, falling into step quite naturally. Carles hated that he couldn't stop himself from asking, "So, who was that?" as they walked toward the movie theater. He tried to sound casual; he didn't like to pester Javi about his other friendships, or appear to be too jealous. For all Carles knew, Javi wasn't even sleeping with the man on the motorcycle, whoever he was.

"A friend," was all Javi said.

So Carles was forced to leave it at that, much as he suddenly wanted to ask a dozen further questions, and depending on the answers to those, perhaps a thousand more. But he held his tongue, trying to quell the nervous tightness he felt across his chest as his mind raced through various possible scenarios and speculations.

Carles tried to reassure himself, telling himself: Javi does not need to tell me who this man is, even if it's not Beckham. This man is not a threat to me. Javi is entitled to have other friends. He is even entitled to have other lovers. The same as I am. It does not mean he doesn't still care for me. And it will help nothing to create a scene out of what might turn out to have the most mundane and simple explanation. The last thing Carles wanted was to create a rift between himself and Javi.

So they walked, companionably, up the hill toward the cinema.

"I always feel bad when I walk up Montera," Javi commented.

The statement surprised Carles. "Why is that?" he asked.

"Because of the prostitutes," Javi answered. "Their desperation. And the way everyone treats them like shit. I mean the transsexual ones have a lot of courage, and I'll bet no one ever tells them so. These are people who have made a tremendous sacrifice, not just in money and pain and parts of their bodies, but in giving up an accepted place in society. People look down on them much more than they do on the ugliest man or woman. And so they wind up selling their bodies—'*dos polvos tres mil*,' one offered the other night, when Enrique and I were walking home—because they're willing to do anything they need to to be able to live their lives as a different gender from the one they were born as. And how many of the people who walk up and down this street every day ever stop to consider them and what they must have gone through to wind up where they are? Who ever stops to think of them as fellow human beings instead of an annoyance to be avoided when they come on to you? It's really kind of sad. Especially since, when they come up to me, I'm usually no different, I don't want to get involved, I just want them to leave me alone."

Carles felt like a complete heel. Here he'd been, caught up in his own little dramas, feeling such negative things about his lover because he didn't know if Javi were having sex with the man on the motorcycle and wondering if the rumors about Beckham being gay were really true and if the man on the motorcycle was in fact the celebrity—as if these concerns really mattered in the context of the world at large. And Javi, meanwhile, had been struggling with such noble thoughts and dilemmas all the while Carles, walking right beside him, had been thinking of him as if he were a brute controlled only by his baser instincts. As if Javi had to be shallow simply because he was so beautiful.

Carles had no idea how to respond to his boyfriend's recent meditations. So he put his arm about Javi and kissed his neck and said, "Did you know I love you?"

"Too heavy?" Javi asked, lightly.

"Not at all, very profound. But I had no idea what else to say. You said so many things, and I would've felt stupid to just say 'You're right.' As if I hadn't been paying attention or something."

"Oh, I don't know. I think it's a basic part of human nature never to get tired of hearing people tell you that you're right."

Carles gave Javi's shoulder a squeeze, and they both laughed. They joined the queue for the Cines Acteon and stood quietly for a time, neither feeling the need to fill up the silence with chatter. Carles looked at the posters for the films currently showing, at the people around him, and at Javi, then at the prostitutes across the street, who made him reflect on the nature of humility. But his thoughts soon drifted to more human and mundane concerns.

He was looking forward to seeing *American Beauty*, it had gotten good reviews as a satire of culture in the U.S. and almost everyone he knew who'd seen it had liked it and recommended it. But his stomach wished they were standing on line for the Palazzo in Sol instead. The salty tang of the popcorn they would eat, which Carles could taste already tingling on the tip of his tongue, was an entirely different craving from that for the sweet rich taste of mint ice cream melting further back in the mouth, leaving the chocolate chunks like rocks jutting up from the shore when the tide pulled back.

Carles felt a sudden wave of nostalgia for the ocean, which always made him remember his childhood. At this time of year, they would be going to the beach almost every day. Carles had a vividly clear memory of eating a Kinder chocolate egg on the beach, and his delight at finding that the surprise inside was a tiny plastic boat. It had been a perfect moment to his ten year old self, like a promising omen that had been sent specially for him.

The ocean was so far away, living in Madrid—not just the physical kilometers separating him from the coast, but the vast emotional distance he'd traveled from who he'd been when he lived in Alcoi. He could get into a car and drive to the ocean, drive, even, to Alcoi, if he wanted to, he could not ever return to the person he had been back then. Even if he'd wanted to. Life moved on. Like the inexorable motion of the tides.

The line slowly moved forward. Carles glanced across the street, then commented, "Usually, what I feel, walking down Montera, is fear. Although I'm never certain if I'm more afraid of the prostitutes themselves or their Moroccan pimps."

"I bought a piece of baklava at the falafel stand once, and

you could tell it made them all so nervous to have a stranger in their midst. I don't even think it was because I was gay, they might not have even known. It was more that I was someone who wasn't one of them."

"I was walking back from shopping at Zara and Pull & Bear last week, just browsing, and as I was coming up the hill one prostitute began to just wail this other woman in the face. I couldn't understand a word she was screaming, just the woman she kept hitting, who kept crying 'Leave me alone.' That was it, just 'Leave me alone.' I couldn't understand why she just stood there, she didn't even fight back, only tried to protect her face with her hands. And even that didn't work, because her face was covered with blood. You could see that her lip had split, and I think her nose was broken as well. And nobody else did anything. Broad daylight. I was afraid to watch too closely, as if I might become the next victim!"

"Even from this side of the street, it sometimes seems like they'll come over and beat you to the ground just for looking at them."

"I wonder, sometimes, if it's worth it for them. I mean, what do they have to look forward to? I imagine sometimes that they must do what they do because they have no other choice."

"Do you think it's so wonderful to be a woman?" Javi asked. "Or was it simply too awful for them to be men?"

Carles was silent for a moment, contemplating those two questions. "I guess that would give one the strength to go through with what they do," he said at last.

They arrived at the ticket counter, and each bought tickets. Then they had to wait on line once again, to buy refreshments. But soon enough they were clutching their popcorn and drinks and walking down the theater aisle, looking for two seats together as close to the center as possible. As Carles scanned the empty spaces, he tried to calculate which was preferable: being in a row closer to the center of the theater but seated at one end of it, or being in the center of a row even if it were closer to the screen? Javi seemed not to deliberate. Unerringly, he walked down to the row smack dab in the center of the theater and, begging the pardon of the people seated there already, started making his way to the left. There were two seats together, fourth and fifth in, that Carles hadn't seen. He should have known something would turn up for Javi, it always did, even though it always surprised Carles each time it happened.

The lights dimmed just as they settled back into their seats, and the trailers and advertisements began to play. It was once again the way the world seemed to be dancing attendance on Javi, Carles thought.

He reached for Javi's hand in the semi-darkness, and Javi responded, turning to look at him for a moment as their fingers intertwined. Javi smiled, and gave Carles' hand a squeeze, then turned his attention back to the screen.

Carles stared a moment longer at this beautiful young man who held his hand, illuminated by the blue light from the screen as if he were bathed in a heavenly radiance. It didn't matter who else Javi might be sleeping with, even if it was in fact David Beckham. The fact remained that Javi was his boyfriend, and that was something wonderful.

Passersby

Carles was staring at two tall, muscular men who stood chatting in what sounded like German just below the balcony. They must be tourists staying at one of the hostals upstairs, Carles thought. He wasn't the only one staring at the foreigners; they were getting appreciative glances from other passersby as well, and Carles enjoyed trying to guess which of the men would look back over their shoulders once they'd passed, and which ones the Germans would turn to look at.

The act of cruising was one of the things that Carles found so invigorating about being a gay man and living in what was so often called the gay "ghetto". Even though none of these men stopped to talk to one another, he thought as he stepped back inside, the outpouring of active sexual interest from cruising created an atmosphere that buoyed one, made you glad to be gay.

They were in the apartment of La Prohibida, one of Spain's most-glamorous and successful drag queens, who was working at a restaurant in Valencia singing cabaret but had come back to Madrid that afternoon for a few days. Carles was never certain whether to still refer to drag queens as "she" even when they were not dressed as women. But since they'd run into Luis and his friends Mario and Tolo standing just inside the Eagle—a haven for the archetypes of macho—Carles figured masculine pronouns were appropriate for now. Luis certainly looked perfectly masculine, if too modern for the Eagle's leather-and-denim dresscode, in a pair of knaki shorts and a beige short-sleeved collared shirt that he'd intentionally mis-buttoned so that it gaped open and displayed his well-built chest. It was only after they had all been talking for some time that Carles realized that Luis' eyebrows were plucked and delicately curved, and that his arms were shaved as smoothly as his chest.

Carles knew the others only casually; they were friends of Javi's. And since he and Javi had simply been taking a Sunday afternoon stroll, when Luis suggested that they all go back to his apartment so he could show off some photos, it was as good an idea as any to Carles. They were an entertaining group to hang around with; it was as if Luis were performing at all times. Carles often felt he played a vital role: audience.

Luis was showing them favorite scenes from different movies, half of which starred Sara Montiel. "You have to see this, too," he was saying, forwarding *La Tonta Del Bote* until he arrived at the right spot. "It's such a classic of Spanish cinema. Just watch how they treat her when she spills the supper."

"And how plastic the food looks, too," Tolo added, having watched the scene a thousand times already with Luis. "I would've thrown that on the floor rather than eat it, too."

Ouside, someone began shouting up at the balcony, and Carles went back out to look. It was for the transsexuals next door; an attractive man Carles often saw sitting in the window at Mama Inés or eating at Marsot. "Buy me a pack of cigarettes before you come up," the blonde was shouting down to him.

"I don't have money on me," he answered, "I just came from the gym."

"Wait, let me get my purse." She disappeared into the apartment, her darker-haired friend (or roommate?) waiting on the balcony, as if to make sure the boy didn't get away. A moment later the blonde was back, fumbling around in a large blue purse until she found a thousand peseta bill.

She cocked back her arm to throw it down to him, but a bus was coming up Hortaleza and created a huge draft in its wake.

"You can't throw that, it'll blow away," Carles told her.

"Don't you have any *monedas*?" the man on the street called up to her.

"This is all I have!" the blonde cried.

"Wait," Carles told her, and he ducked back inside the apartment. Luis had recently washed his laundry, and it was still hung on an indoor rack to dry. He carried a clothespin out to the balcony, and passed it to the blonde.

"Gracias," she said, clipping it to the bill and dropping it to the man waiting below. Then she and her dark-haired companion both went inside to wait for the gym-bunny and the cigarettes.

Tolo stepped out onto the balcony with Carles, and they began to comment on the passersby, starting with the two blonds directly beneath them. "Pity the poor vegetarians who pass up those two sausages!" Tolo said.

Carles laughed. "Most of the vegetarians I know still eat carne *viva*. And those two definitely look like they'd deliver a mouthful."

"Well, fuck dieting, if it comes to those two, I believe in snacking between meals."

Carles nodded across the street. "That mountain of muscle who tries to be so butch is definitely an exclusive bottom," he said.

"Is this firsthand knowledge, *cariño*?" Tolo asked.

"Secondhand. My friend Miguel Angel—"

"Miguel Angel? Then it's a trustworthy source, at least if it has to do with sex."

Carles felt a curious mix of surprise and jealousy, that Miguel Angel had such a widesperead reputation. But then, Madrid was a pueblo, in many ways, especially within the gay scene.

"Poor Miguel Angel," Tolo continued. "He must've been so disillusioned to get that musclefeast into bed only to discover they were both passive!"

"Hola! Bon soir!"

Tolo tapped Carles' shoulder. "Looks like you've managed to score," he said, pointing to the other sidewalk, where a man was jumping up and down and wildly waving up at their balcony. With a start, Carles realized it was the crazy Frenchman from the supermarket; he'd forgotten that the man had told him he was staying at the Hispano, two floors above them.

"Quelle sorpresa!" the man shouted up at them, and crossed to the near sidewalk, obviously intending to continue a conversation. Carles wanted to dash back inside and hide, before anyone noticed that he was talking to this man; it would be just his luck for someone he knew to walk past right now. But he was afraid the man would just keep shouting for him and create an even worse scene.

"Hola Christophe," Carles said, with absolutely no enthusiasm. The Frenchman, by contrast, positively glowed when Carles called him by name.

"Who is it?" Luis called out to them from inside the apartment, not wanting to miss any gossip.

Tolo answered, over his shoulder so as not to miss any of the action, "Carles is showing me how to pick up men from the balcony. He seems to have quite a gift for it."

"Let me see!" Luis shouted, rushing out to join them on the

balcony and look down at Christophe. "Hola!" Luis called down, waving grandly. Then in a stage whisper to Carles, "Are you sure that's the one you want? Why don't we invite those two tall blond men up instead and have an orgy?"

Christophe energetically cried "Hola!" back at Luis.

"I didn't pick him," Carles insisted, "he picked me." Javi had joined them, squeezing out onto the tiny balcony to see what all the fuss was about. "Remember that crazy Frenchman I told you about," Carles explained, "who tried to pick me up in the supermarket of El Corte Ingles?"

"Love among the eggplants!" Luis exclaimed. He stared at the backs of the two German men, who had begun to walk down toward Gran Via, then looked up and down the street, making sure there was nothing else of interest about. "Well, have fun," he told Carles, and then went back into the apartment.

"¿Como estás?" Christophe shouted up at them.

"I didn't do anything to encourage him," Carles explained to Javi. "But he won't take no for an answer."

"You're just a heartbreaker," Javi told him. Then he leaned over the balcony and shouted down at Christophe, "This is my boyfriend! Leave him alone, do you hear?"

The transsexuals who lived next door rushed out onto their balcony to see what the commotion was. "You tell him," the blonde one told Javi.

"Men are such pigs," the other one said, "trying to steal other people's boyfriends." She shouted down at Christophe, "Cerdo!"

And then, having had their say, the two of them went back into their apartment and turned up the volume on Cher's "Believe."

Christophe meanwhile was staring up at Javi, who'd put his arms around Carles. "Tu novio," he said, spreading his hands in that universal gesture that meant 'I come in peace, and I'm holding no weapons.' "Tu novio," he repeated, "yo entiendo." And he disappeared inside, presumably to go upstairs to his room and lick his wounds.

"My savior!" Carles said, pulling Javi closer and kissing him on the lips.

"Now that the drama's over," Luis said, "you just have to see this next scene." The others, including Javi, followed him inside, but Carles remained on the balcony, his embarrassment replaced by a feeling of contentment that Javi had laid claim to him so publicly.

The blonde next door came out onto the balcony to look down on the street, and hesitated when she saw Carles still there. He felt he should withdraw—after all, she lived there, and he was only visiting—but then she smiled.

"I'm sorry," the blonde said, "but my friend didn't bring back the clothes pin."

Carles wondered when the man had come back, somehow missing all the excitement. Was he still inside their apartment, with the dark-haired one?

"Don't worry," Carles said. Although losing a friend's clothes pin was exactly the kind of thing that Carles himself worried about excessively.

"Want a cigarette?" she said, holding out the newly-purchased pack toward him.

"Thanks." Carles took one, even though they were Ducados and he preferred lighter tobacco. It was the polite thing to do.

The Night is Young

"Are we going to spend all night here?" JuanMa complained.

Carles tolerated Javi's friends, but sometimes they got on his nerves. JuanMa was perhaps the one who most aggravated Carles; he was constantly bitching and complaining. His every statement seemed to have a bite to it, and as a result Carles always felt on the defensive when he was around him, as if he were constantly awaiting when the next ambush or attack would come. It made it hard to relax. JuanMa had bleached hair that was moussed into little peaks, and always looked as if he was dressed in an outfit purchased on one of his visits to Javi at work.

"What's wrong with it?" Rocio asked, looking around them. They were at Why Not? with its curious arched ceiling, like being in a subway tunnel. "There's men for all of us to pick from here."

Rocio was a tiny little spitfire who'd been friends with the rest of them since early high school, when she decided nothing could be cooler than to hang out with the gay kids. So she'd been tagging along with them to discos and gay bars, and fighting playfully with them for boys. She liked to flirt outrageously with everyone, and often seemed to be more sexually aggressive than any of the others. When arguing over whether or not a cute boy was gay or straight, Rocio would often summon the guy in question over to them and ask him point-blank. If the guy was gay, she'd literally hand him over to one of the others, as if it were a fait accompli that sparks would fly; if he were straight she'd triumphantly crow "I told you so!" And quite often, her triumphs regarding these men didn't stop there...

"Where do you want to go?" Raul asked.

Raul was one of the quieter friends in the group. He worked at Madrid Rock, and wore retro clothes that came from one of the second hand shops. He wore his sideburns long and had a little mosca just below his lower lip and generally got along with everyone.

"It's not that I want to go anywhere in particular," JuanMa said. "But I want to find Nacho before we go to Ohm."

Nacho was their usual drug dealer, at least for cocaine and pills. Hashish came from someone who delivered it to Raul at the store, and he parceled it out from there.

Often, Carles was surprised that Javi had grown up in the heart of Madrid, hanging out in Plaza Chueca with these people and going to nightclubs since he was in his mid teens. There was an air of innocence about Javi that made him seem like he must have grown up in a pueblo somewhere distant from any big city, somewhere protected, where values and morals were as natural as sun and rain and growing things.

It seemed like cheating somehow for him to have grown up surrounded by so much depravity and vice and not to have been corrupted. Because Javi, for all the sex he had and the all-night partying and the drinking and the drugs he took, seemed to exist apart from it all somehow. He did all those things simply because they felt good, without the desperate urgency that JuaMa had for getting high or Miguel Angel did for finding sex, that insatiable craving that was never fulfilled. It was one of the most appealing things about Javi, Carles sometimes thought, his being a part of this sordid world but seeming to rise above it. Carles envied that trait of his lover's, for he often felt the appeal of many of these things—wild sex, losing oneself to drinking or drugs—but was afraid of his own responses to them, of the lack of control, of how he felt afterwards. Javi seemed to feel no shame or regret for anything he did.

Rocio looked at her watch. "Do you think Nacho might still be at Mama Inés?"

"I don't know," JuanMa said. "Maybe we should go to Star's Café, even though it's too early, and wait to see if he shows up there."

"Doesn't he have a mobile?" Carles couldn't help asking.

JuanMa gave him a pitying look, and Carles knew he had asked a foolish question. He hated how Javi's friends often made him feel so old and out-of-things. He wasn't modern enough for them, he didn't understand anything. "Like we bring our mobiles with us when we go out," JuanMa sneered.

Carles felt less foolish about his question after all. He'd simply been considering the problem from the wrong perspective.

Yes, logically, he told himself, but he knew better than to say anything. It wasn't worthwhile, and his own restraint let him feel a bit superior to these youngsters who were so full of themselves. They would grow up someday, Carles told himself.

The group spread out as they walked between bars, Carles found himself walking next to Javi. They were alone for a moment, as if the crowds of people out on the street on a Friday night made them seem more private rather than the reverse. They were hidden in the anonymity of general revelry, instead of the specific scrutiny of Javi's or Carles' friends.

Carles linked his arm through his lover's, as if they were some honeymooning couple. "Shall we go to see *Krampack* tomorrow night, after you get off work?"

"I'm sorry, *cariño*, but I can't. I've already got plans for tomorrow night."

Once again Javi didn't mention any further details.

Carles felt a moment's rage. He felt Javi slipping away from him, that he was only getting half of Javi and he wanted more. Hell, he deserved more. Was he not Javi's boyfriend? The man on the motorcycle was just an affair, a romantic idyll. But it didn't really mean anything more.

Or did it?

Should Carles put his foot down? Confront Javi about this other affair he was maintaining and ask if it was serious, if it was a threat to their own relationship? He hated to provoke fights, in general, he was more the peacemaker sort who wanted everyone to be happy than the kind who rocked the boat. At least, unless the boat in question was political, and had to do with a lack of rights for homosexuals. But that was different, it wasn't personal. It was personally important, but it wasn't urgent in the same way his relationship with Javi was. And when it came to his personal life, Carles was someone who didn't like change.

But the change he was most afraid of just then was losing Javi. Which gave him strength to ask, casually, "Oh, who with?"

Once he had committed himself, he was full of regrets. Did he really want to know the answer? Of course, Javi couldn't just say outright that it was David Beckham. He would say his friend on the motorcycle from the other day. Even though Javi had not introduced him to said man on the motorcycle.

"Remember that friend of Igone's who came over to the apartment last week, who was just promoted to Igone's job?" Carles nodded. "I ran into her the other day and agreed to spend some time with her and her boyfriend."

Carles felt so relieved and so embarrassed at the same time. He felt so guilty for thinking the worst of Javi, when he'd been so wrong. Of course Javi was entitled to have his own friends and to spend time with them and he didn't need to report in to Carles about who he was seeing and what they were doing together. And Javi had a wide circle of friends, of all sorts. He was so easy-going and charming, he could start talking to anyone and they immediately accepted him and trusted him. And Javi, too, was very trusting, almost innocently so. Carles sometimes worried that he'd come to harm of some sort by being too trusting, but then Javi always did seem to have a charmed life. And Carles could benefit from loosening up a bit, to not analyze every single action and reaction so minutely and simply live his life.

Nonetheless, Carles was still a bit resentful that Javi would spend his time with some strangers instead of spending it with him.

"She seemed nice," Carles said. "What are you going to do? Why don't you see if they want to go see *Krampáck*, too?" He paused, feeling as if he were being too pushy. "Or would you rather be alone with them?"

"Actually, I think they'd rather be alone with me," Javi admitted.

Carles' jealousy blossomed anew. "You mean..."

"Well, she did mention wanting to see what it was like."

"Have you ever done that before? I mean, with a man and a woman."

"No," Javi said. "That's why I thought it might be interesting to give it a try."

Carles felt his control of the situation begin to slip. He'd leapt out of the frying pan, directly into the fire. As if the man on the motorcycle hadn't been enough for Carles to worry about.

Independence

It was that subtle mysterious moment when cuddling became foreplay. Javi tilted his head from where he nestled into Carles' shoulder as they watched TV on the couch, and looked up at Carles. And then they were kissing, their hands flying to each other's face, thigh, shoulder, neck. After-dinner drowsiness was forgotten. *Cronicas Marcianas* was forgotten, though Xavier Serdà kept talking and making jokes for all those many viewers across Spain who were not currently distracted. But in Carles' apartment, only the two of them existed, and their mutual passion and desire for one another.

Carles released Javi's mouth only long enough to lift Javi's shirt over his head, then began kissing him again, tongue seeking tongue while Javi's arms were still stretched above him, caught in the fabric. One hand fell free, and sank to cup Carles' cheek and pull him forward, as if they might somehow become joined more closely through sheer force of will. The other hand came free, and Carles let the shirt drop behind him.

There was a clank, as a spoon hit the floor, knocked over by the falling shirt.

The lovers paused, laughed, looked at what had happened. The remains of the dinner Carles had cooked lay on the table, waiting to be cleared away and washed up. A bowl from which they'd eaten ice cream had been tipped over, and Javi reached out to right it, but that was all. Carles stood and slid the table back from the couch, then undid the drawstring on his shorts and let them fall to the floor. Summer clothes were so convenient that way. He removed his shirt and stepped free of his clothes, but before he could rejoin Javi on the couch his lover had grabbed hold of either hip and began to lick from Carles' navel out toward his flank. Javi threw one arm about Carles' back, squeezing him gently, while the other hand forced Carles' legs apart and lightly feathered their way up and down his inner thighs. Carles groaned.

What was it, he wondered, that made something so simple feel so good just because Javi was the person doing it? When had he ever had so many nerve endings in his belly, just where Javi's tongue was moving? How had they all lain dormant for so many years, until just this moment? What had he done to deserve to be so lucky?

Carles bent, pressing his lips to Javi's, slowly sinking down until they were both again seated on the couch. He clawed at Javi's pants, wanting them off, rubbing Javi's cock through the fabric while he waited for his lover to unzip them, to be naked as he was, to be ready and available. Javi's body was wonderfully familiar to Carles, but it had never become comfortable; simply to touch it, to hold him, still sent a thrill through Carles. No matter how much he worried about his lover's other affairs, when they were together the chemistry always overrode all his concerns. Carles hoped this would never change, even though he didn't understand it. He wanted always to find Javi so exciting, so alluring, so desirable. Which wasn't difficult to imagine; he couldn't contemplate ever failing to find Javi sexy.

Because they were so familiar with each other and each

other's bodies, there was neither order nor score keeping to their lovemaking. That was one of the wonderful things about an ongoing relationship. It wasn't like a new encounter, where if he sucks your cock there's a social obligation to return the favor. There wasn't that feeling that he was doing you a favor. It was simply pleasure. And if Javi remained dressed, either partly or in full, while giving Carles pleasure, there was no rush to finish him off, for his turn to follow. It would come when it came, or not, and that was all fine. They could go from foreplay to sex and back again, doing only what they liked and wanted to do just then. So often, Carles thought, when you picked up someone new, it felt like you were following a script or trying to complete a scavenger hunt, having to pass through certain acts in a certain order before allowing yourself to claim the goal of orgasm.

Javi still hadn't removed his shorts. He pushed Carles back and began to suck his cock, no longer the coy teasing licks of Carles' abdomen a few moments earlier. So much of sex was anticipation, teasing, offering, but holding back. But that was only one side of sex. There was also the more animal urgency, the grunting, thrusting, physical lust of sex. Of losing oneself so completely in another person that the two bodies became one.

It had been difficult for Carles to learn how to accept pleasure. To just enjoy it, without offering anything back, which was his stronger instinct. To accept that Javi might be enjoying the act of giving him pleasure more than anything Carles could do to him just then.

He still struggled with himself over this issue. Especially with Javi. With other men, it was easier to accept if they wanted to do all the work, as it were, for a while. But with Javi he wanted always to show his devotion, to be the one giving pleasure, making his lover feel special.

Carles stood and lifted Javi with him, unzipping Javi's shorts and pulling him into the bedroom. They lay down on the bed and reached for each other. Carles rolled atop of Javi, interlocking their legs as he kissed his lover's neck and shoulders. Soon would come that decisive moment, when one or the other of them would assume a role, even if later they flipped. It was one of the aspects of gay sex that always fascinated Carles, the fluidity of dominance and submission between two essentially equal entities, as opposed to heterosexual intercourse where the man would always wind up topping the woman, from biological necessity. With two men, the dynamic was always changing, even if one (or both) partners had a strong preference for one position or the other. But everything was possible.

Javi held Carles' cock and squeezed it tightly. "I want you to fuck me," he said.

There were condoms and lube in the nightstand. Carles reached for the drawer, grabbed a foil packet, tore it open. But before he put it on Carles reached for Javi, dragging him forward so that Javi's crotch was positioned by his head. He took Javi's cock into his mouth and only then, sucking gently, did he begin to unfold the condom onto his own dick. Without releasing Javi's cock, Carles then squirted a dollop of lube into his hand and began to work it into Javi's ass, spreading it over his fingers and then slowly, one by one, poking them up inside Javi, loosening him up. Javi's body always responded instantly; Carles, on the other hand, often needed more time to relax, to get used to the width of one finger, then two, working upward before he was ready for someone's cock. As a result, he liked to go slow, giving his partner time if it was needed. For one thing, it gave Carles time to think about, to get ready for, what was to come.

Javi pulled back, straddling Carles chest and then sliding backward, toward Carles' cock. And in a moment they were joined, Carles thrusting upward as Javi sank back onto him. They both paused, as if the shock of connection had overwhelmed their senses, then Carles began to grind his hips slowly, gyrating. Sometimes Carles would lie utterly still as Javi lifted himself up and then down along his shaft, sometimes it was Javi who remained frozen mid-squat as Carles pushed his hips upward again and again. Sometimes one or the other asked for a pause, to catch their breath, to not cum too quickly. But soon they'd start to move again, building up to that inexorable fall into bliss.

"I'm going to cum," Javi said, as he drew too near to the precipice of orgasm. Carles grabbed Javi's cock and began to tug on it as he thrust up inside his lover. Suddenly, Javi's cock convulsed in Carles' grasp, shooting out a jet of white semen across Carles' chest. Its hot wetness, falling against his skin in spurts, sent Carles into orgasm as well, and he cried out as his own cum shot into the condom's plastic reservoir tip.

They lay entwined in a sweaty heap, Carles' cock still lodged inside Javi. He began to soften, but still stayed more than half-hard. He worried that he should pull out, and take off the condom properly, wipe himself off. But he didn't want to move. His cock was so sensitive, even Javi's gentle breathing sent shivers through him, as their bodies shifted slightly.

Carles smiled with delight, and kissed Javi desperately, as if he were afraid that it was all a dream that Javi was his boyfriend and he would soon wake up. Javi returned the kiss, and suddenly their bodies broke apart. They lay together, caressing one another's bodies and kissing.

At last, Javi pushed himself off the bed and stood up. "Do you want to shower with me? I promised I'd meet JuanMa and Victor by 2:30."

"You're going out?" Carles asked. He tried not to feel hurt. But he couldn't help asking himself, why wasn't he enough for Javi? What was Javi looking for, that he wasn't satisfied with what they'd just shared, the way Carles was?

Carles stayed in bed while Javi showered and got ready to

go out with his friends. They would go drinking, they would take drugs of various sorts, they would go dancing. Would Javi have sex with someone else tonight? Carles tried not to think about that, but after he'd brushed his teeth and climbed back into bed, he couldn't help returning to the subject, his mind refusing to stop worrying and let him sink into sleep.

Javi might wind up having sex with someone in the backroom at a disco, high on ecstasy and alcohol and letting feelings take control. He might go back with some man to the guy's apartment and have sex there, maybe spending the night but probably not. But as upset as Carles might be by these possibilities, they didn't really mean anything, being simply actions of the moment than anything more serious.

But now that he had his own place, Javi could bring someone home with him. And if the man spent the night, they'd perhaps talk the morning after. As if it were the beginning of a relationship.

"I've never had a chance to be on my own," Javi had argued, when he told Carles that he was moving out from his family's home. "I don't want to just trade living with my parents for living with you. I need to see what it's like to have my own place."

Intellectually Carles understood, but he still felt hurt. On one level it felt like a rebuff, both of himself and their relationship. He had to keep reminding himself that Javi was nearly a decade younger than him, and wasn't necessarily ready for the same things that he was.

It was also difficult to be too hard on Javi when his reasons for moving out were so altruistic: Javi's older sister Lola had returned home unexpectedly with her eighteen-month-old baby. She'd been unable to put up with her husband's abuse any longer, especially when in a drink-enhanced foul mood one night he'd actually raised a hand at their daughter because the baby wouldn't stop crying. She'd put herself between his fists and their child, and the following morning, when he was supposedly out looking for a job, she took little Brenda and a suitcase full of clothes, and took the bus back to Madrid. Her parents had, of course, made room for her, but it was cramped with all of them living there; it simply wasn't set up to accommodate so many people, the way the larger apartment they'd had when Lola and Javi were younger had been.

The evening following her return, Lola and Javi were sitting in Chez Pomme trying to figure out what she would do with her life now. Much as her mother would've preferred that her children stayed home to eat dinner, they couldn't really talk with their parents around. Lola had needed their comforting and acceptance, but she also needed a less judgmental point of view on how to rebuild her life. And she'd needed a break from constantly tending to the baby. So their parents had agreed to watch Brenda, and the siblings had set aside their rivalry and sat down together over a meal like two adults—albeit young ones—trying to come up with a practical solution.

Javi offered to give Lola his room and look for an apartment, saying that it would be necessary for her to have their Mother there to take care of the baby, especially if Lola was thinking of working, which she'd have to do at some point.

One of the waitresses overheard them and mentioned that there was a room suddenly free in her apartment, giving Javi the telephone number of her roommate Igone in case he were interested in coming to see it. This was the kind of thing that always happened to Javi. He seemed to evoke that sort of response from people, strangers even, as if he were a lost puppy that needed protection. It was easy for them to fall under the spell of his good looks and easy charm. But more it was that situations seemed to resolve themselves for him without any apparent effort on Javi's part. He put his faith in the world, and the world, unexpectedly Carles thought, treated him with good faith in return. He was touched by a glamour. Sometimes Carles couldn't believe his own good fortune in being Javi's boyfriend. He was often shocked by his own jealousy of Javi, a sense of envy for his beauty and his manner and the way people responded to him, which tried to express itself by a desire for Carles to control his lover. Which was often hard for Carles to fight against.

It was a constant internal struggle: to be Javi's loving boyfriend but not try to possess him too much. Because Javi was one of those elusive beautiful creatures that would be smothered by a cage, be it emotional or physical. So Carles tried to give them as much space as possible in their relationship. They had an open relationship, sexually, even though Carles was horribly jealous of every man who Javi even spoke with. But as an ex-lover of his had explained once, when Carles was newly coming out himself, how could he deny someone he loved anything, especially pleasure. And for all the torment each new liaison evoked in Carles, his elation each time Javi returned to him was all the more intense.

Carles had his own little adventures and histories on the side, as well, sometimes out of desperation on nights when Javi was off with other men, sometimes out of a sense of moral determination to live a modern, plural lifestyle unconstricted by the antiquated heteronormative ideals of mainstream societies. Sometimes simply because the sex was convenient and appealing.

But he would give it all up for Javi, he knew. Without a moment's regret. If only Javi would make the same sacrifice for him. But Javi wouldn't even consent to live together. Not yet, at least... Carles hoped that eventually Javi would change. Once he'd had time to spread his wings and fly on his own for a bit.

When he thought about the future, Carles often liked to imagine his life like a page out of the IKEA catalogue: two handsome well-dressed men in a domestic ecstasy. They have nothing overt in the adverts to signal that they're gay—no pink triangles or rainbow flags—but you can feel the subtle sexual tension between them, the knowledge of each other's bodies. They're domestic without losing their masculine edge. That's what made the images so sexy for Carles.

Carles had gone with Javi to IKEA to help him select items to furnish his new place. Because Javi was moving into a flat where other people already lived, he was only furnishing a small part of an apartment—basically just his own rooms. But they wandered the entire store, to get a feel for possibilities and prices. To make sure there weren't any low-cost gems hidden further along the path, strategically placed so that one had already made a more-expensive choice earlier on... And then they went back, and looked again at the items they'd made note of on the special sheets of paper that were so handily provided everywhere.

Shopping for furniture is different than any other kind of shopping. Furniture is so much about the future. Food is so temporal, even the canned stuff—technology has forestalled decay, but the products have their expiration dates clearly labeled. And clothing, too, has a lifespan; even something "classic" in style is not expected to last forever without wearing out. But one doesn't really think of using up one's furniture or outliving it, mostly one sheds it whenever one moves. Otherwise, it seems almost impossible to get rid of. Carles thought of the hideous red chair in his parents' home, that had belonged to his grandmother. All the little knick-knacks his parents had accumulated over the years and never pared back.

Fashion is about what's new, what's hot. It's a constant out with the old, in with the new cycle. And when it ran out of ideas, it had no shame about going back to whatever had been trendy a few decades ago, and calling it retro, and charging top prices for it.

In a way, it hurt Carles for them to go shopping together, as if it were their shared future they were shopping for, when it was actually Javi's independence they were setting up. Especially watching countless pairs of gay men of all types—gym bunnies and well-dressed *pijos* and pathetic dweebs and even the occasional leathermen—buy "family sized" comforters and mattresses and the like, while Javi wanted everything in "individual" sizes.

When it came time for Javi to want things in "family sizes" would Carles be the man he wanted to share those items with?

Suddenly Carles remembered the man on the motorcycle he saw Javi riding with the other day. The one who never took off his helmet. The one who, at the time, he'd felt certain was David Beckham, since he'd just been listening to Miguel Angel go on about a rumor he'd heard that David Beckham was having a gay affair.

It was one thing to gossip about whether or not a celebrity might be gay, but Carles hardly ever tried to imagine Beckham or anyone else actually engaged in the act of sex with another man. His fantasies usually involved memories of sex he had actually had, or imagining sex with his lover or men he'd already been involved with. Miguel Angel, on the other hand, was sure to have done so; Carles sometimes wondered if Miguel Angel could think about any man without imagining what he would be like in bed. He wondered, sometimes, if Miguel Angel had had these same thoughts about Carles himself. It seemed strange, given Miguel Angel's aggressive sexual appetite, that they hadn't ever wound up having sex together, but their friendship never seemed to take that particular turn. Maybe because of Manfred. Manfred wouldn't have been upset if they had sex, but because Manfred was always there, even if in the background, as Miguel Angel's boyfriend, Carles had never considered Miguel Angel as truly being available. Not in the sense that Carles needed. Because he couldn't easily separate sex from the possibility of something more, and Miguel Angel didn't offer anything more; anyone might get sex from him, but Manfred had all his affection.

Miguel Angel sometimes joked that Carles was the one man left in Madrid who he'd not had sex with, although that was perhaps debatable. One night, a few months after they'd met, he and Miguel Angel had wound up in a curious threesome at the Strong Center. There had, of course, been some sexual tension between them—was it ever possible for gay men to be friends without some tension?—but they'd never acted on it. In the back room, each had gone off in pursuit of his own pleasure, in separate areas. But they'd run into each other again, in the darkness, and were comparing experiences when a flash of light revealed a man standing nearby, with his cock in his hand. It was an impressive cock, and they each felt moved by it.

Miguel Angel immediately sat down and took the man's dick in his mouth. Carles, feeling awkward at watching his friend fellate this stranger, began to play with the man's nipples. He felt almost as if he couldn't just leave—not that Miguel Angel would notice or be upset—but they'd been in the middle of conversation and it just didn't seem...polite.

Besides, the man's cock truly was impressive.

The stranger began kissing Carles, and when Miguel Angel stood up and told the man he wanted to go into a *cabina* for the guy to fuck him, the stranger grabbed Carles' hand and pulled him along, too. Carles didn't really do much, mostly just encouraging the other two. At one point, Miguel Angel was rimming the other man, who in turn unzipped Carles' pants and began to suck his cock. But Carles didn't have any sexual contact directly with Miguel Angel, it was all via the other man.

Carles was pretty sure Miguel Angel didn't really consider him as a sexual possibility, not any longer. But he was equally certain that Miguel Angel did so for just about every other man he met, and this would hold especially true for any celebrity, even ones he only saw in photos.

But Carles lacked the practice of such extrapolation; when he fantasized, he usually remembered sex he'd already had, or sex he'd seen, whether as a voyeur in real life at a sauna or in two dimensions in videos and magazines.

Would Beckham be a top or a bottom? The rumors never mentioned that when they said someone or other was gay, which probably proved that they were just rumors; a gay man wouldn't leave out important details like that when he was gossiping about who—and what—he'd done.

Carles tried to picture Beckham having sex with his boyfriend, Beckham wrapping Javi in his broad embrace and kissing him, Javi responding. What would it be like? How would it be different from the sex he and Javi had just had? That was the question Carles always came back to: What did another man give Javi that he couldn't?

To his surprise, Carles found that his dick was painfully hard, even though he'd just cum so recently. He began to stroke himself slowly, imagining Beckham's hand on Javi's cock.

A moment later he was cuming again, short white spurts falling across his belly.

He felt guilty for a moment, as if his fantasy had been unfaithful to Javi. But that didn't make sense, since Javi had been part of the fantasy. The sex had been between Javi and Beckham, Carles had merely been watching. What did that mean? He was too tired to think about it. He leaned out of bed and kicked the light switch off.

Eyes closed, exhausted after two orgasms so close together, Carles let himself drift off, conjuring a vision of Javi's beautiful face to sweeten his dreams. "Javi," he whispered, and for a moment he wasn't sure if it was his own voice or Beckham's who'd uttered that name. And then sleep claimed him, and he no longer worried.